UNFORGETTABLE

ALSO BY LORETTA ELLSWORTH

In a Heartbeat

UNFORGETTABLE

Loretta Ellsworth

Walker & Company
New York

YA
811
C·1

First published in the United States of America in September 2011
by Walker Publishing Company, Inc., a division of Bloomsbury Publishing, Inc.
www.bloomsburyteens.com

For information about permission to reproduce selections from this book, write to
Permissions, Walker BFYR, 175 Fifth Avenue, New York, New York 10010

Library of Congress Cataloging-in-Publication Data
Ellsworth, Loretta.
Unforgettable / Loretta Ellsworth.
p.   cm.
Summary: When Baxter Green was three years old he developed a condition that
causes him to remember absolutely everything, and now that he is fifteen, he and
his mother have moved to Minnesota to escape her criminal boyfriend and, Baxter
hopes, to reconnect with a girl he has been thinking about since kindergarten.
ISBN 978-0-8027-2305-5
[1. Memory—Fiction. 2. Impersonation—Fiction. 3. Dating (Social customs)—
Fiction. 4. High schools—Fiction. 5. Schools—Fiction.] I. Title.
PZ7.E4783Un 2011   [Fic]—dc22   2010049590

Book design by Regina Roff
Typeset by Westchester Book Composition
Printed in the U.S.A. by Quad/Graphics, Fairfield, Pennsylvania
2   3   4   5   6   7   8   9   10

All papers used by Bloomsbury Publishing, Inc., are natural, recyclable products
made from wood grown in well-managed forests. The manufacturing processes
conform to the environmental regulations of the country of origin.

For my sister, Monica, who fills my life with laughter;
and for Betty Smith, keeper of the family memories

I WANDER'D lonely as a cloud
That floats on high o'er vales and hills,
When all at once I saw a crowd,
A host, of golden daffodils;
Beside the lake, beneath the trees,
Fluttering and dancing in the breeze.
—William Wordsworth

UNFORGETTABLE

Twelve Years Ago

It's a warm spring day when Mom takes me to the play-ground near our apartment. I jump on the swings and kick my three-year-old legs and soar as high as I can, until I think I'm going to flip over the top and come back down the other side.

"Don't go so high," Mom calls. She looks small from up here. I'm big and not afraid. I puff out my chest and let go of one side of the swings to wave at her. *See? I'm fine.*

But in that instant I lose my grip and slip backward. It happens so fast I don't have time to react. I fall and land on my head in the indentation of dirt and sand under the swing. When I wake up I'm surrounded by Mom and a bunch of other people. In the distance the sound of a siren closes in. I'm scared and embarrassed, but I'm told I only suffered a minor concussion and don't even have to stay in the hospital overnight.

Mom tells me all this later because I don't remember anything about the accident. I don't remember much before that, either. But something happened that day, because soon after, I started experiencing voices in unusual ways, like Mrs. Wheeler next door who sounded like bacon sizzling, or Halle Phillips, my best friend from kindergarten, who sounded like yellow daffodils, or my dad, who sounded like a quiet stream.

And something else happened, too, because ever since that day I've remembered *everything*, as though my memory somehow got stuck in the "on" position. I remember the starchy scrambled eggs I ate for breakfast three weeks later, and the contents listed on the back of a cereal box that I read five years after that. I remember the pain from gashing my hand on a piece of broken glass when I was four and having stitches. I remember Halle and how she cried on September 23 because she'd just lost her front tooth, and how I told her she was pretty. I remember how she hated Tater Tots and I said I did, too.

I remember my dad helping me ride a two-wheeled bike when I was three and a half, how he adjusted the training wheels when it leaned to the left, and how afterward it leaned to the right. I remember two months after that, how Mom sat me down on the plaid sofa, how she ran her finger along the pattern as she tried to find a way to tell me that Dad had been in an accident. I remember feeling my heart stop in that instant when she said he was dead, as if I'd died, too, but then it started beating again, even though it hurt and I had to put my hand on it to ease the pain.

That same feeling washes over me whenever the memory of it pops uncontrollably into my head, maybe during a movie or a stroll on the beach, or in the middle of math class. And I'm back there, experiencing it all over again, and I put my hand on my heart and feel it break a little bit more each time.

I'm lucky in a way. I have four months of memories of my dad. I can still recall the scent of his aftershave all these years later; I can see his greenish-blue eyes and his quiet smile. I can remember Halle, even though she moved away after kindergarten. I remember her daffodil voice and her pigtails pulled so tight that it looked like her face hurt.

I've never misplaced a shoe, lost a library book, or forgotten a homework assignment. But there's a downside. Not all memories are good. That's why last month when I blew out the candles on my cake for my fifteenth birthday, I only had one wish. I wished I could forget.

How We End Up in Minnesota

Imagine remembering every day of your life as though it just happened. Halle is as fresh in my mind today as she was ten years ago. I kissed her three days before she moved. We were on the playground in the middle of the monkey bars; Halle was hanging across from me by her arms and I caught her off guard. I grabbed her shoulders and planted a big kiss on her lips when she was looking the other way. She almost fell, then she wiped her mouth off and climbed up the bars away from me. She tasted like milk and Oreo cookies, our snack that day.

And now I'm here at her school and even though we haven't seen each other since kindergarten I can't picture her looking like any of the girls I see in the hallway. They smell like hairspray and perfume and cigarettes and they wear low-cut tops that show off their curvy figures. Of course Halle must have changed. I know that. But I haven't looked her up yet because

I'm a gutless coward. What if I've walked past her ten times already? How would I know? My heart does one of those little flip-flop things just thinking about it.

Mr. Shaw places the quiz facedown on my desk. I turn over the top corner and peek at it, expecting a B. I inhale a short breath when I see a red C-minus, with a note next to it: *Talk to me after class.*

Brad Soberg hoots when he gets his quiz. He's a farm kid twice my size, but he's 90 percent muscle from moving hay bales around his barn and lining up dairy cows for milking. He pumps a solid fist in the air next to me. "B-plus!"

Mr. Shaw nods from across the room. "Don't get too excited. I always grade easy on the first quiz, since it's a review of what you learned last year."

Brad looks over at me. He has a better chance of getting milk out of me than seeing my score. C-minus! Is anyone else looking? I feel as if the grade is written on my forehead in red ink. It's the lowest grade I've ever gotten. Of course, I haven't been in a regular school for three years, either. I crumple the test into my backpack and look out the window. Mr. Shaw's room faces the parking lot of Madison High. It's 2:36, four minutes before the bell is supposed to ring. A row of twelve buses is already lined up outside in a diagonal pattern, like yellow dominoes waiting to be tipped over. My bus is number thirty-three and it's the second bus from the right. Three years ago I rode bus number four and the year before that I rode bus number two. In kindergarten I rode bus number fourteen and I always sat in the fifth seat from the front on the left-hand side.

Mr. Shaw's voice brings me back to the stuffy classroom.

Even with the window open, a stagnant odor of sweat and old books fills the room. That triggers memories of my fifth-grade track-and-field day when I placed fifth in the long jump and Kent Herzog placed fourth, and Stevie Kessler placed third, and . . .

Gotta stop this. Dr. Anderson thinks the wiring in my brain changed when I fell off the swing all those years ago. That's the only explanation he can come up with for the free-floating memories that crowd my head. I concentrate on my watch, an atomic solar quartz wristwatch, and soon the memory eases and I'm thinking of Halle again, who's the reason I'm in Minnesota. At least part of the reason.

"Your assignment is to read the first three chapters of *The Great Gatsby* for tomorrow," Mr. Shaw announces. "And don't be surprised if there's another pop quiz."

I'm not used to this place, to the swarm of bodies and books in the hallways. My head swirls and I try to stay focused and in the present. It's hard with the memories pressing in, triggered by random thoughts and smells and sounds. There's a constant battle in my head over past and present. Too often, the past wins.

For most people, memory is like sand. It shifts and settles over the open spaces of the mind, piling memory on top of memory until what's left is a fragile sand castle in the brain, one that will crack and leak out all the old memories when the flood of new ones pours in. But my memory is like stone. It's hard and permanent, and most of all, it's always present, a living monument to my own history.

The bell rings and I wait until everyone else has left before

I approach Mr. Shaw's desk. He looks up and hands me a piece of yellow paper with writing on it.

"Since you're new this year, Baxter, I've arranged for a student to be your study buddy the first couple of months."

Mr. Shaw's voice is a tall pine, deep and woodsy.

"Are you talking about a tutor?" I croak. "I had an off day. I can do better."

"This isn't a punishment, Baxter. I think it's nice to start off ninth grade with a friend to help you study. Are you open to that?"

"Uh, sure." What can I say? That I got carried away marking the letter C on my exam? I take the note and stick it inside my copy of *The Great Gatsby*.

Mr. Shaw flashes an easy smile. He's one of those teachers who wears blue jeans and a T-shirt to school. His beard is long and thick. He could be mistaken for the janitor except for the lanyard around his neck that all the teachers wear. "So how do you like Minnesota so far?"

I consider how to answer that. Wellington is two hundred miles north of Minneapolis, and it feels isolated up here, as though you're in a different country altogether. The roads cut through forests of pines and lakes and man-made hills of reddish dirt, full of deer flies and mosquitoes. The woman who rented us our house bragged about the new Dairy Queen in town. "It's warmer than I thought it would be for a town with a sign advertising Polar Bear Days," I say.

He lets out a low whistle. "Wait a couple weeks. This is about as far away from Southern California as you can get."

That was the plan. Get as far away from Dink as possible. He's the main reason we moved here. My mind flits back to three years ago, when I testified against him. Now he's out of prison. Moving all the way to northern Minnesota may have gotten him out of sight, but he's never out of my mind. I shiver just thinking about him.

"I'll let you go so you don't miss your bus," Mr. Shaw says. "If you have any questions or problems, feel free to talk to me."

"Thanks." I'd rather face the deer flies. I hurry to catch the bus and sit alone.

I should be enjoying this, being in school again, but Dink ruins it. He's like the Boogeyman who I was afraid of when I was little, but back then he didn't have a face and I didn't know his name was Dink. Mom said that he'll be on probation for a long time and can't leave California. He doesn't know where we moved, and there's a restraining order. But a restraining order doesn't stop the Boogeyman.

So I can't help but look over my shoulder on the walk home from the bus stop. The two sophomore girls walking behind me think I'm checking them out because I keep looking back. They giggle and whisper, so I focus on the street in front of me until I reach our townhouse, then jog up the driveway. I flash a quick look at the street before I open the door. The two girls both burst into laughter.

I plop my backpack on the kitchen table. There's a note on the fridge under a red magnet that says, *Frozen pizza. Be home at seven.*

The nice thing to do would be to wait for Mom, but I'm starved, so I turn on the oven and find the pizza pan. Unpacked boxes line the wall. One of them holds the spice rack, but Mom packed the kitchen and I don't know which box it's in. I'm too lazy to search for it now, so I'll have to eat my pizza without chives.

While the oven is preheating, I pour a glass of juice, open my backpack, and take out the Gatsby book. The yellow note sticks out the top. Mr. Shaw's handwriting is fast and messy but the name pops out at me: Halle Phillips! My heart skips a beat, and I'm back in kindergarten. It's Monday, February 23. Halle drew a horse with two heads. I told her that if a horse had two heads, it would die. That made her cry. A month later she told me she was moving. That made me cry.

Mom thinks we moved to Wellington on a whim. It was 5:47 p.m. on August 14. She'd closed her eyes and poked her index finger at a spot on the map of the US that I held in front of her. But I moved the map right before she put her finger down. I remembered that Halle had moved to Wellington, Minnesota. I didn't know if she was still there, but I liked the thought of finding out. Besides, Mom's finger was pointing toward North Dakota, and I figured Minnesota had to be better. Mom let out a shriek of delight. "I've always wanted to see snow," she said, and three weeks later we're renting this townhouse and I'm enrolled at Madison High School.

My life is moving so fast it makes my head spin. Mom already has a job as a waitress at the Tin Cup Restaurant—not her ideal job by any means, but it's a job. And we're far away from Dink.

What are the odds that on the second day of school you're assigned the girl of your dreams—well, the kindergarten version of the girl of your dreams—as a tutor before you've even had a chance to look her up? And what if she's not the girl I remember? What if she's changed into someone completely different from the girl from Pascal Elementary who confessed that her favorite color was yellow because I wore a yellow shirt to school that day?

She might not even remember my name. As hard as I find that concept to be, most people don't remember their classmates throughout the years. I'm counting on that. Because the last thing I want is for Halle Phillips to remember Baxter Green, the Memory Boy.

Why Dink Wants to Kill Me

At first Dink didn't seem like a bad guy. But in the end his true self came out. Maybe he has a "jerk" gene in him. Maybe he just gave in to his own greed.

When I met Dink I was eleven going on twelve. He brought me a puzzle—a pirate one that was too easy for me. He gave Mom a dozen roses. He wore a suit and he told dumb jokes that made her giggle. I tried not to worry too much, even though he sounded like muddy water and he had a shapeless chin.

Mom and I lived in a small house three blocks from the overpass. The constant whoosh of traffic was background noise. Mom sold advertising for the local newspaper and money was always tight.

So when Dink took Mom to fancy restaurants and drove his beat-up metallic green Camaro that he thought was flashy,

Mom fell hard for him. I didn't know what to think, though I wanted Mom to be happy because she hadn't dated much since Dad died. I didn't want to be a worrier. But three months later when Dink moved in I had this uneasy feeling, like we were sinking in quicksand.

The pieces of Dink didn't fit together. He said he worked in executive sales in the communication industry but he had these scary gargoyle tattoos on his upper arm that you didn't see unless he was sleeveless. He had excuses for never having any money and Mom had to pay for everything.

Still, I tried to like him. But when Dink told me he was going to take me to a movie and later backed out, all the great things my dad did with me before he died popped into my head, and Dink couldn't compete with my memories. Mom finally took me to the movie, and when we returned I recited my favorite scenes word for word.

"See what you missed?" Mom said.

Dink stared at me. "How'd you do that?"

Mom smiled. "Baxter has a fantastic memory."

Dink was so fascinated with my abilities that he had me look at a piece of paper with a bunch of numbers for five seconds and asked if I could memorize them. No problem.

"I can't believe this," he said. "What's your trick?"

I told him that when he flashed the paper in front of me I took a mental picture of it, then when he asked me the numbers I found the picture in my memory and recited what was on it. Dink's mouth dropped open as though a light bulb had turned on in his head.

"That's like a photographic memory or something. You're

a genius, Baxter!" Even though I was still mad at him, the praise made me feel good. My memory wasn't getting me in trouble like it did in school, when I corrected my teachers and sounded like a know-it-all. After that Dink acted really nice. He even bought me a guitar and said he'd teach me how to play it.

One day Dink asked me to go for a ride with him. "I want to show Baxter where I work," he told Mom. But when we got in the car, he said he needed me for a project. "Top secret," he said, "so don't tell your mom or anyone else."

It was Sunday and the place was empty, but Dink had a key. Two other guys came and Dink introduced me like I was a star or something. Everyone was excited to meet me.

Dink had me sit at a computer terminal. "Just watch the numbers. They'll go by really fast. Remember as many numbers as you can, but they have to be in order. You understand?"

"Yeah," I said. "What is this for?"

"You're saving the company a lot of money by doing this, Buddy. They'll probably send you a nice gift certificate." He patted me on the back, kind of hard.

I played with the buttons on my shirt, stalling. "I don't know, Dink."

His eyes narrowed. "You said you'd help me, Baxter. You're not going to wimp out on me now, are you?"

"I think I should ask Mom first."

"I thought this was going to be our guy thing, just between the two of us. You have to stop being a momma's boy and stand on your own two feet. You're not a baby."

So I did it. Reluctantly. The numbers flew by like a speeding train. After I watched them flash across the screen, Dink asked me to write them down, or as many as I could remember.

I wanted to trust Dink, but something was wrong. The air felt electric, the way the men's eyes were on me and how they kept watching the doors. A few hours later, when my fingers were so stiff I could barely move them, Dink said to stop. He took the pieces of paper with the numbers written on them and went into a room with the other men for a long time. Their voices were muted. When they came out, Dink was smiling. The men left through the back door and Dink took me home.

"You did good, Baxter. So good that we might use you again next month. But this has to stay between us, okay? Remember, it's a guy thing."

I nodded, but I felt like I couldn't breathe. I moped around for two weeks until Mom said something to me, which made Dink give me a nasty look behind her back. I was starting to think that Dink wasn't such a nice guy. He now had money to fix up his Camaro but he still didn't help with the rent. He spent a lot of time in the spare bedroom that he'd turned into an office. He didn't take Mom to fancy restaurants anymore.

The next month Dink took me to his workplace again. The same two guys were there. But this time it was all business. They acted edgy and no one high-fived me or gave me compliments.

Dink sat me down in front of the same computer. "Okay, Buddy, let's get to work."

"I don't want to do it," I said. "I want to go home."

Dink glared at me and his hand pushed down hard on my shoulder. "You're going to do *exactly* what I tell you to do."

And that's when I realized that Dink had a jerk gene in him, like the fruit flies I read about who were bred for aggression. It just took a while for Dink's gene to kick in.

A few weeks later I was looking for a pencil and I went into Dink's home office, even though I wasn't allowed in there. I found a pencil at the back of the drawer, but right next to it was a large envelope full of money. It was filled with one-hundred dollar bills, six hundred fifty-three of them. All together, there was sixty-five thousand, three hundred fifty-eight dollars inside. And underneath the money were copies of the pieces of paper with the numbers I'd written down.

I didn't know what to think. I was scared. That same week Dink was arrested for stealing credit card numbers from his work. When the police came to our house, I hid under my bed. I thought they'd arrest me for helping Dink, but instead they asked me a lot of questions. When I told them what Dink had me do, Mom hugged me and said sorry about a million times. I gave the police the pieces of paper with the numbers I'd written.

Mom thinks we're safe here. But Dink is no longer in prison and I know he wants to kill me for testifying against him. Plus there's something that even Mom doesn't know about. I took Dink's envelope full of money.

Hiding My Stash

I'm watching *The Andy Griffith Show* on the oldies channel when Mom comes home. It's the episode where his son Opie accidentally kills a mother bird and raises the babies, and then Andy tells Opie he has to set them free. I've always thought that my dad would have been like Andy: wise and caring, someone who would help me raise baby birds.

Mom pauses in the hallway between the kitchen and living room. She hangs her purse on the doorknob to the basement, a cavernous place that could fit our whole apartment from California. We've never had a basement before and I'm not sure what you use it for other than storing the furnace. Mom nods toward the television. "Haven't you seen that episode a hundred times?"

"Sixteen."

"You have it memorized. Why watch it again?"

"This way I can laugh in advance." Just because I memorized the show the first time I watched it doesn't mean I enjoy it any less the sixteenth time. "Would you say my dad was like Andy Griffith?"

She shakes her head and her top lip curls up. "He was more like Barney Fife."

Barney is Andy's inept assistant. He's the funny one who always messes things up that Andy makes right again. Barney cracks me up, but I'm not sure he's father material.

She sighs. "Your dad was great. I just don't want you thinking he was some kind of god. He was a good guy, but he had his faults."

I want to mention that nobody could be worse than Dink— he would have killed Opie's baby birds without a thought. But I don't really want to talk about Dink, and I know Mom doesn't want to talk about Dad *or* Dink. Either one brings up sad memories.

"How was school?" she asks.

"Mr. Shaw assigned me a study buddy."

"What's that?"

"It's basically a tutor. I got a C-minus on my first English test."

"You always get As in English. How could you possibly get a C-minus with your remarkable memory?"

By selecting the letter C for every answer. I shouldn't have told her about the tutor or the grade. How am I going to make a fresh start if I act the same way I did before? I shrug. "I haven't been in a regular school for three years, Mom. I'll do better next time."

She shakes her head. "I guess no one is going to suspect you of being the Memory Boy when you're struggling in class. But really, Baxter. C-minus? You can do better than that."

I don't mention that my tutor is an old classmate from California. No use making Mom worry before the spice rack is even unpacked. "How was work?"

Mom runs a hand through her chin-length blond hair. It used to go halfway down her back, but then she cut it as part of her fresh-start approach to our new life in Minnesota. Her fingers stop abruptly when she comes to the end, as if they're searching for the rest of her hair.

"Turns out I'm pretty good at waitressing. We have this guy, Mr. Schneider, who orders the same thing every day: toast, tea, and eggs over easy. Today I messed up and accidentally gave him the wrong order, a bacon omelet. Thought he'd be mad, but guess what? He loved it. Says he's going to order that every day from now on. You know, this isn't so different from selling newspaper ads. It's really all about people skills."

I flinch at the words "people skills." Most people think I'm an obnoxious know-it-all. But that was the old Baxter. The new Baxter is an average guy who gets C-minuses on his tests.

I'd never mess up and give someone the wrong order. But Mom did and it ended up better than if she hadn't. It's these unexpected twists in life that nag at me; how making a minor mistake or change can yield such different results. Like getting a C-minus and winding up with the tutor of my dreams.

Mom takes in the mess of boxes lining the kitchen wall. "I hate moving." She reaches into the pocket of her white apron streaked with ketchup and coffee stains and takes out a pack of Winston Ultra Lights. She flicks out a cigarette and sticks it in her mouth, raising the lighter to the tip in one fluid motion.

"What happened to the patches I bought you?"

She scrunches up her face. "They make me nauseous."

"Nauseous is better than dead."

"I'm cutting down. I just moved two thousand miles and started a new job. Give me a break."

"Dink smoked, too."

She puts up her hand. "We agreed not to talk about him, Baxter. I know I shouldn't smoke. I'll go outside. Honestly, one smoke, that's all I'm asking for. This is only my second one today." She waves the pack in front of her. "They're Lights. Doesn't that count for something?"

She turns and walks out the back door.

She hates my nagging, but if it guilts her down to two cigarettes a day, I'll keep at it.

I go back and forth between being angry at her for bringing Dink into our lives and feeling bad for her. She was so shocked that Dink turned out to be a thief and all-around jerk. And she tried to make it up to me. When school became unbearable, she worked out a deal with Dr. Anderson, a memory researcher at the Institute who was interested in studying me. They hired a tutor for me and I didn't have to attend school anymore. Life became tolerable again.

I pull out the scrap of paper resting inside my right pants pocket. Dr. Anderson wrote down his phone number before we moved, then chuckled when he gave it to me. "You obviously don't need it written down. Habit, I guess." I like the note in my pocket, though. It's something a guy with a normal memory would carry. I think of calling Dr. Anderson now, but it's only been a few weeks. I wonder if he's found a new brain to study or if he misses me. After three years of attending weekly sessions at his research facility, I felt more comfortable talking to him than to the shrink Mom sent me to, Ms. Rupe, who insisted that I talk about my memories, which was like replaying them over and over again in my head. As if *that* helped.

Mom is outside flicking ashes on the pavement. It's been a whole week since I checked my stash, but I still feel like a gambler who compulsively counts his chips. I go to my room and open the closet. Stuffed in the back, behind cardboard boxes and piles of clothes, is my guitar case. But there's no guitar. It still smells like guitar, though, and it's filled with mementos from my life: books, pictures, stuffed animals, a margarine container full of shells I found at the beach. Having these things helps me somehow. They make my memories real.

Near the back of the case is a bulging white envelope that contains sixty-five thousand, three hundred fifty-eight dollars, all in crisp bills held together with a rubber band. There was ninety-seven cents in the ashtray on Dink's desk and I took that, too. It was an impulse reaction that seemed right at the time.

Later I worried what would happen if I turned it in, if I would get in trouble. So I've never spent any of it, not even the ninety-seven cents. The coins jingle at the bottom of the envelope.

If Mom knew, she'd say it's not right to keep it. But I still say Dink owes us.

I put the guitar case back in my closet and go into the

living room. Mom is still outside. The newspapers tagged me the Memory Boy when it was discovered that I'd written six hundred credit and debit card numbers from memory after viewing them as they flashed across a computer screen. I'm the kid who can memorize a phone book or a thick novel because I don't forget anything once I see or hear it. I don't forget anything.

Most people are impressed by that. They don't know how crowded my head feels or what a curse it is. Plus there are too many Dinks in the world who see me as a way to cheat the system.

It's nice being in school again with other kids, doing the same work as them, even if it's just to read three chapters of *The Great Gatsby*. But Dink lurks around every corner. The memories pop up more often; his heavy brows that furrowed at the least little thing, his receding hairline, and the sneer he reserved for me when Mom wasn't watching.

Even when Dink isn't here, he's here, like a disease that won't go away. And like the disease he is, I know I need to find a cure. Dr. Anderson thinks that if I fill my head with new memories at a new school I'll figure out a way to get rid of him. But Dr. Anderson doesn't know about the money. And he doesn't know Dink.

The Sound of Daffodils

The bus pulls up three minutes early today. There are usually four of us at the corner—the two girls who laughed at me and a sophomore guy with short-cropped hair, but the girls aren't here yet.

"I'm getting my license in a couple months," the guy tells me as he rocks back and forth on his heels. It's become a mantra. He says it every day, as though he's ashamed to be riding the bus.

I tug at my jeans, which are too loose because I've grown three inches this summer and it's either wear them too big in the waist or walk around in high-water jeans. I tower over the guy and I wonder if that's why he keeps reminding me he's older.

Since today is my first meeting with Halle, I sit in the fifth seat from the front on the left-hand side, just like I did in kindergarten. Maybe it will bring me good luck. The guy sits in the back with the other sophomores. The driver peers around for the two girls and revs the engine. He has a gray beard and a permanent scowl on his face.

"We're missing two. They're late. Hope they didn't sleep in or they'll be walking today."

"You're three minutes early," I say. "Yesterday you came at 7:38."

The driver lifts the bill of his cap and stares back at me through the mirror. "Is that so? I was here the exact same time yesterday. Maybe your watch is slow."

I shake my head. "Not possible."

His eyes become slits. "I don't make mistakes with time, kid."

I open my mouth and close it. The guy doesn't understand. Time is important. Or rather, the keeping of time. I may not be able to control the flood of memories, but I can at least make sure they're accurate. I want to inform him that there's no way my watch is slow, that it receives daily time-calibration radio signals and is accurate to less than a second a day. I want to tell him that he's wrong and he's probably left kids stranded at bus stops all over town because of his inability to keep accurate time.

The old Baxter would have told him all that. The old Baxter also would have gotten kicked off the bus. Instead I jab my pencil into the vinyl seat in front of me when the driver isn't looking. Blurting out random information has always been a problem for me. But the Memory Boy persona is not what I'm aiming for at my new school.

Ninety seconds later, which always seems longer when you're

sitting on a bus with the driver shooting daggered looks back at you, two figures hurry down the road, waving their arms and jostling backpacks.

"You're late," the driver says when they finally make it to the bus. "Next time I might not be here waiting."

I just shake my head. The driver's voice is sour milk.

"Sorry," the girls say in unison, but they're smiling. The bus lurches forward and the girl in the white jacket almost falls on top of me. The bus driver smirks in the mirror as they land in the seat behind me.

"That guy is such a jerk," one of them says.

"I hate riding the bus," the other one says.

I turn around. "He wanted to leave you, but I made him wait."

"Thanks," white jacket says. "You're new, aren't you?"

"Yeah."

"You're a freshman, right?" the other one asks. Both of them have straight, brown hair and identical jackets, but her jacket is black.

"Yeah." I want to say that I'm from California because that might impress them and God knows I need to say something impressive to make up for yesterday, but then they might ask what school I went to before or why I moved here and pretty soon I'd be telling lies upon lies, and I hate lying. I'd have to remember the lie forever and that goes against my grain of remembering things accurately.

"Cool. I like your tan," she says, then they start talking to each other like I don't exist. After feeling awkward for fifteen seconds, I turn back around. I could tell them that the bus was three minutes early today and that they might need to start out earlier tomorrow or the same thing will happen again, but I don't say anything. Being a know-it-all never helped me win a lot of friends back at Pascal Elementary.

I haven't made a ton of friends yet, but it's only the third day of school. Brad Soberg sat with me at lunch the first day, and yesterday a guy I remember from Geometry roll call as Bennet comma Kevin sat across from me. "How's it going?" he said, then ate the rest of his chicken sandwich in silence.

It's not like I thought I'd be one of the cool kids. Well, maybe that possibility made a cameo in my mind when I imagined this new life in a town that's less than a hundred miles from the Canadian border. I thought that being from the land of movie stars and beaches might make me at least appear to be cool. But the first day of school erased any hopes of that happening when I saw the football and hockey jocks pushing freshmen guys in the hallway, and some of those freshmen guys had forty pounds on me and wore letter jackets.

Now I've readjusted the dream to just fitting in and having a few friends and not thinking about Dink, if that's even possible. And not letting anyone find out about my past or my memory. Reinventing yourself is harder than I thought, especially when you don't like to lie about your past. And especially when the past keeps getting in the way.

But hope springs eternal, and today I'm seeing Halle Phillips again.

Halle Phillips, who once brought a shark tooth for Show and Tell from her trip to Florida, then a postcard from that same place the next day, and the following week she brought a picture of her grandpa, and after that her favorite candy—green jelly beans, which she shared with our class; and . . . my head swims as more memories fight their way up. I focus on my watch, staring at the dials like Dr. Anderson taught me until I can push the memories back down. Sometimes it works. Other times it's like trying to turn off a running faucet by using a broken spigot.

When I look up I'm the last one on the bus. The driver is glaring back at me. "You going in or do you plan on spending your whole day here?"

I grab my backpack and leap out of the bus without touching the steps. The door closes immediately behind me and I'm standing in front of a three-story building with a faded brick exterior the color of ash. As far away as we are from California, I still have this sick feeling that I'm going to turn around and see Dink standing behind me. Or maybe he'll be waiting in the parking lot with a loaded pistol. I feel safer in large groups, so I join the flow of students into the school, being careful to stay in the middle, and I have just enough time to go to my locker before the first bell rings.

We haven't had any assignments yet in Science class; we've just spent the past two days taking notes from the overhead projector. I open my five-subject notebook and copy the outline, although it's a pain to do. I mean, what's the point? But I'd look like a slacker if I didn't, so I scribble away like everyone else. At least taking notes helps kill time until I see Halle and keeps me from getting too anxious. Once I tried an exercise with Dr. Anderson where I wrote down my memories and then burned the paper as a means of getting rid of them. It didn't work.

I have two more classes after Science, and the morning drags by. The clocks are slow in all the classrooms and that bugs me, so I avoid looking at them or I'll be tempted to get up on a chair and adjust the time.

At 11:06 I hurry from homeroom, a twenty-five minute study hall that most students use for catching up with friends. I show Mrs. Algren my pass and wait at a small table in the middle of the library, which is also the computer center.

I have an empty piece of paper in front of me, a sharpened number-two pencil, and my copy of *Gatsby* open facedown. To say that I'm nervous is an understatement.

I size up every girl who enters the library; first, a thin girl with glasses and long, blond hair. She's laughing and clinging to a guy so I doubt that's Halle. Another girl with black hair and black lipstick and red streaks in her hair. She passes me without making eye contact.

I hold my book in the air as two more girls enter the library. They smile at me in a friendly way but walk by. At 11:12 another girl enters. She zones in on the book at my table and walks purposefully toward me. I focus on her face for any hint of recognition. Nothing is familiar in any obvious way. She has light brown hair instead of blond pigtails like the Halle Phillips I used to know. A red barrette holds back her bangs. The ends of her hair brush the top of her shoulders. She's way too beautiful to be the girl I remember. The Halle Phillips I knew had a button nose and her knee socks kept falling down. This girl has a sloped nose that turns up at the end, high cheek-bones, and a curvy waist. In fact, she has far more curves than the Halle Phillips I knew, but then again, kindergartners don't have curves. She's wearing a short skirt and her long legs are sockless.

"I'm Halle," she says.

It's the same girl but everything about her is different. For one thing, she's hot. But it's her voice that makes me lean forward. She still sounds like yellow daffodils, sweet and creamy and fresh. My own voice catches and I creak out a small "Hi, I'm Baxter."

She sits down across from me and points at my book. "One thing you need to know is that everyone says Shaw's class is hard, but he's one of the most respected teachers here. And once you figure out how to take his tests, you won't have a problem. So don't freak out that you got a bad score on the first one."

I nod, still taking in the scent of her voice.

"My sister had him, and he doesn't ask the mundane questions like 'What color is Daisy's hair?' or 'How big is Gatsby's pool?' So don't stress out on memorizing trivial details. I mean, he might ask how Nick is related to Daisy, something fundamental, but the rest of the test will be essay questions that make you think about what you read. So you should be reading for comprehension and looking at the meaning behind the words."

She stops and studies me like she's trying to place me. It's suddenly hot in here. A drop of sweat cascades down the inside of my shirt and settles in my navel.

The look is replaced by a frown. "You did read the first three chapters, didn't you? Because I'm not wasting my time helping you if you're a jock who thinks I'm going to be doing all your work while you dribble a ball down the court or practice your tennis serve."

"I read it," I assure her, although I'm flattered that she thinks I might be a jock. She obviously doesn't remember me from Pascal Elementary. Even in kindergarten I couldn't hold on to a ball.

She crinkles her nose. "Sorry, bad experience with my ex. I don't mean to take it out on you. Anyway, the important thing is to take good notes during Shaw's discussions. And read the chapters. If you get stuck, we can find a quiet spot to read out loud, but I'd prefer you read it ahead of time. Does this time work for you?"

"It's perfect." She's perfect.

"Mr. Shaw said you're new. Where did you move from?"

My heart quickens at the thought of how to answer. If I say California, will that be enough to connect the dots in her head? But my teachers know that I'm from California, and I don't want to start our first meeting by lying outright to her. In the end I decide to take a chance. California is a big state, after all.

"I'm from California."

"Really? I used to live in California when I was little. But seriously, you should know that surviving Shaw's class will be nothing compared to surviving the winter in northern Minnesota. It's freaking cold here and we get a ton of snow."

"Fifty-six inches, on average."

Her eyes widen.

"Um . . . I looked it up," I say with a nervous laugh.

She stands and picks up her books. "You're going to lose that bronze tan, you know, and then you'll look just like the rest of us albinos from the North Country. We'll start tomorrow. Same time, same place."

And then she's gone, like a swift breeze moving through the California heat, leaving me refreshed and wanting more.

I'm still swimming in the scent of her voice, strong and lasting. As much as I hate the constant refrain of memories that play like a marathon in my head, there are some moments worth remembering. This is one of them.

How I Measure Up

The meeting with Halle is a break from worrying about Dink, who hovers like an invisible cloud in my life. Seeing her again and hearing her voice lets loose the rampant memories of kindergarten. After she leaves I let them flow: how I missed my mom and held on to her leg the first day of school, those feelings of anxiety before I made a friend, every hurt and fear as well as every moment of joy and excitement. There's my teacher Mrs. Skrove giving me a hug; she smelled like glue sticks and she smiled at me and nodded when I recited lines of conversation I'd heard on the bus.

"You have an amazing memory," she told me.

"I appreciate you remembering that it's Patrick's turn to go first," she said the next day, not even getting mad that I interrupted her.

I'm still reliving my kindergarten days when I realize that

the library has emptied and lunch period is half over. My stomach lets out a disappointed growl so I jog down to the lunchroom and grab a plate of nachos, then sit next to Brad Soberg from Lit class. He asks, "Hey, can I have a few?" and even though I don't want to share, I do anyway because Brad doesn't leave me stranded after he's finished eating his hamburger and fries.

"Do you know Halle Phillips?" I ask him.

"You bet," he says. "Why? You like her?"

I avoid his question. "She's my tutor."

He picks up a chip and a line of cheese stretches down to the plate. "Lucky dude. How'd you manage that? She and her boyfriend broke up just before school started."

"Mr. Shaw assigned her to me."

He laughs. "That almost makes it worth failing his class. She is kinda out there, though."

"What do you mean?"

He talks between mouthfuls. It's a good thing they're not skimpy on the chips or I'd starve today. "She's gone green."

"Green?"

"She's all about global warming, recycling, saving the environment, that sort of stuff."

Maybe it's because I'm from California, but that doesn't sound too "out there." It makes her seem even hotter.

"Last year in junior high someone smashed open the pop machine and left a note that read, 'Give us healthy drinks.' They never caught anyone, but we all knew it was her."

He takes a long slurp of his milk. "But if you can get past

all that, go for it. You should make good use of that private time with her. She won't be on the open market for long."

Brad makes her sound like a piece of meat. But he's right. What great luck for me that she just broke up with her boyfriend and that I have her to myself for half an hour every day.

But is she out of my league? Am I the type of guy girls even think about? A girl who sits across from me in math wrote "possible prom date" with a question mark next to my name when she didn't know I was looking. I could ask Brad's opinion, but asking a guy I just met if he thinks I'm hot will probably get the crap beat out of me.

Halle thinks I'm too dumb to pass Lit class. Does Halle go for dumb guys? What if she likes smart guys? Could I risk exposing my memory? It's the third day of school and I'm already facing an inner struggle between wanting to impress Halle Phillips and keeping my memory secret.

"Speak of the devil." Brad nods at a tall guy making his way across the lunchroom. The crowd parts like the Red Sea as he walks past, but he's carrying a math book instead of a staff. He has that athlete physique: buff and muscular, tall with blond hair and a confident smile.

"Hunter Austin, future hockey pro."

"So he's Halle's ex. And he's smart?"

"Don't let the book fool you. It's more prop than anything. Not that he has to be smart."

"Why not?"

"He's a hockey god. Hockey reigns supreme up here," Brad informs me. "We learn to skate before we walk."

"He doesn't seem like Halle's type."

Brad smirks. "Yeah. Popular jock who's already being recruited by the pros. He's every girl's type."

I make a small fist in a furtive attempt to check out my own pathetic biceps. Brad notices.

"You got the pretty boy thing going for you. Halle likes that. But if you want one of these," he says, flexing a muscle the size of a fence post, "you come to my place."

I have to admit I'm impressed. "You have a weight room at your house?"

"Don't need one. You get this from lifting bales of hay. We could use another hand this fall, if you're interested. Might give you an even playing field with Hunter."

"But she broke up with him."

Brad laughs. "Rumor has it that it was the other way around. Hunter broke up with Halle to date Jenna White but now he's having buyer's remorse. Jenna's a leech. She's already picking out wedding music. I give it a month."

"Does that mean he'll try to get Halle back?"

Brad points a finger in the air. "Score one for the new guy. Question is, will Halle take him back after he dumped her? And of course he hasn't dumped Jenna yet. So you have a small window of opportunity, if you know what I mean."

I never said I liked her, but I guess it's obvious. Why else would I be quizzing Brad about her life?

"So if you think she's hot, why aren't you going after her?" I ask him.

Brad shakes his head. "She's not the type to go for a farm boy who uses agricultural pesticides and is proud of it. Besides,

I have a girlfriend. Alexis lives in Duluth with her mom but spends summers here with her dad."

Even farm boy Brad has a girlfriend. I've never been remotely close to having one. If I'd stayed in school, would things have been different? Not that I had a lot of friends back at Pascal Elementary, where the last two years I got in trouble almost every week for correcting my teachers.

The running documentary of my life back at Pascal Elementary starts to play in my head. It runs for a few minutes and when I finally break free of it, Brad is gone. I didn't even hear him get up or say good-bye. My plate is empty, too.

Dr. Anderson has a quote on his door that reads, "If we remembered everything, we should on most occasions be as ill off as if we remembered nothing." The quote is from William James, a famous psychologist who lived around the turn of the century. His brother was the novelist Henry James and his sister was Alice James, and . . . the bell rings. I'm late for class again.

My California Tutor

"Call me Coyote," he told me the first day we met. His real name was Jack Simmons. I thought I'd be calling him Mr. Simmons. "And we'll be meeting out on the south terrace, so wear sunscreen if you burn easily."

Coyote was a bushy red–haired grad student from Michigan. The Grad Program had run out of assistantship money when he applied, but there was a stipend available to tutor their newest subject, which was me.

I was twelve years old and Dink had just been sentenced. I had some trust issues. I didn't want a tutor. I didn't want to go to school. I didn't want anything other than to be left alone. But adults never listen to what you want.

Jack's goal in life was to get a tan. He told me he thought that if he spent short periods of time in the sun and used sunscreen with a high SPF he'd accomplish that task even though he was a fair-skinned redhead and his previous attempts had always turned his skin lobster red.

"First thing we need to do is figure out what you like," he said, "because nobody studies unless they're rewarded and I'm not about to mess with grades and all that stuff. So we need a system where you study and then get rewarded and I give you all As if you pass your tests. So what do you like?"

I'd never been asked that before. "I like to ride my bike." After Dink was arrested I took long bike rides and I'd pedal as fast as I could, dangerously fast. I don't really know why I did that.

"Cool. I'll see if I can get a couple of bikes for us to use and we'll plan some long rides."

That perked my interest. The Institute was surrounded by curvy, tree-lined roads and steep hills.

So each day we spent two hours studying on the south terrace. I developed a deep tan and Coyote turned a darker shade of pale. On Fridays after I passed my tests we'd go biking through the hills, speeding down winding roads and slowly trudging back up. Sometimes we talked as we biked, but mostly I just felt the wind wrap around me and tried not to remember or think about anything except the road up ahead. Sometimes it worked.

One day I was having trouble with a math assignment. I could always remember the formula, but I was struggling with the application of it. I slammed down my book.

"Can we go riding?"

Coyote looked up from his reading. "It's Tuesday."

"So what?"

"So we ride on Fridays, after you've passed your tests."

"I need to get away. I don't understand this."

Coyote put down his book and looked at my math problem. "You've always had it easy, haven't you? Never had to work to understand material?"

"I guess." Up until now math had been mostly memorization and simple problems. But now I was studying geometry and trying to apply geometric concepts to word problems.

"It was the same for me. I didn't have a super memory like you, but I was so smart I never had to study. Then when I went to college and my classes were harder I didn't know how to study because I'd never needed to before."

He pulled out a sheet of paper. "The best thing I can teach you is how to study. We'll do the first problem together, then you do the rest while I watch."

He guided me through it, showing me how to apply the formula to the problem. I finished the assignment and Coyote felt sorry for me and we rode our bikes afterward for half an hour.

Coyote was the closest thing I had to a friend those three years. I'd lost touch with the few ones I'd had at Pascal Elementary and was beginning to feel like an outcast. Coyote taught me things that had nothing to do with studying. He taught me how to get a soda from the machine with just one quarter, how to play desk football with wads of paper, and how to play poker, which he consistently beat me at. He yelled when I got annoying. He made me feel normal again.

He was also the one who told me I should leave the Institute. "I know you think Dr. Anderson is some kind of god. I'm as big a fan as you are. But you can continue meeting with him *and* go to school. You don't want to miss out on high school," he said. "It's the common American experience, the hell that binds us together, the fact that we all suffer through it and live to tell about it later. You'll regret it if you don't go."

So I planned to switch back to school in tenth grade, but when Dink got out, our plans changed and I went back a year earlier. I miss Coyote and Dr. Anderson, but what I miss most is the bike riding. When I left the Institute I was hoping they'd give me the bike I'd been using, since my old one at home was too small for me. No one ever offered. Mom says she'll buy me a new one when she gets a few paychecks under her belt. In the meantime I have to hoof it.

Coyote also gave me some advice before I left. "Whatever you do, don't raise your hand the first six months at school. Even if you know the answer."

He knew that would be hard for me, so he gave me a piece of tape. "Pretend it's on your mouth when you're tempted," he said.

When I told him we were moving to northern Minnesota he laughed. "With that badass tan and those biker legs, the girls are going to fight over who sits next to you."

There's only one girl I want to sit next to. So far, neither my tan nor my legs have impressed her. And the tape? I keep it in my pocket as a reminder.

Good Dreams versus Bad Dreams

I'm staring at the green wall of my bedroom, unable to sleep. Pushing down memories all day is hard work. At night, when I'm tired, they run rampant, like a dam with a crack in it. The memories seep through when all I want is to shut them off for a while, to escape into the oblivion of quiet. Someday, the whole dam will burst.

On top of that, I worry. A lot. There's Mom, who I worry will die while I'm still young because she smokes behind my back. There's Dink, who I worry will find us. And then who knows what he'll do to me?

Then there's the worry that my brain will leak if I can't find a way to forget, that I'll eventually lose any kind of filter or organization up there, like a library with no Dewey decimal system. The other worry is that I might forget everything; that my brain will kick into reverse and keep going until all that's left is a blur of white noise.

But the reason I can't sleep tonight is because I keep thinking about Halle Phillips's daffodil voice. It floats through my mind and whispers in my ear. When I finally do fall asleep, I dream of that same daffodil voice that I heard in kindergarten, the sassy attitude that went with it, and how she sounds now, how she hasn't changed all that much after all. I dream of her curves and those dark eyes that draw me in. I dream of her long, sexy legs.

When I wake up I want to go back to sleep, to keep dreaming about her. I roll over and look at the clock: two minutes before the beep, which lasts an annoying five seconds and repeats every minute.

Pans rattle in the kitchen and the strong odor of coffee hits my nose. Mom is up. I turn off the alarm and pull the covers over my head. *Five more minutes.* The fog of sleep wraps around my brain.

But my memories are up and forcing their way in. I'm in front of Dink. Dink's muddy voice yells at me.

"We're running out of time. I don't want to hear any more of your crap. You don't have to ask your mom. Do as I tell you, Baxter!"

I sat frozen in front of him, a pencil poised in my hand. Dink was doing something bad. Why did he want me to write down all those numbers?

The next moment a hand cracked across my face. My cheek had a hot streak from where Dink hit me, leaving an imprint. Dink's eyes were wild marbles moving back and forth between me and his two friends.

"You start writing. Now!"

My hand shook as I scribbled down the numbers.

Dink. I can't stand the memories. For three months after he was arrested I'd dream about him and wet the bed. I grab my watch off the nightstand and clutch it in my palm. I pry my eyes open and stare at it, focusing on memories of anyone but Dink.

Dr. Anderson was in front of me. His lab coat was blinding white; he looked like an angel.

"I want to help you figure this out, Baxter. Will you let me help you?"

I reach out to him and my watch falls to the floor. Is this real? Is Dr. Anderson here in my room?

"Baxter, wake up. You'll be late for school." Mom opens the curtains, flooding my face with sunlight. I put up my hand to block it out. When did I fall back asleep? How much was memory and how much was dream?

Is dreaming what it's like to have a normal memory? When you see some things that are real, but not everything is as it seems? Or is it where you unconsciously choose to discard memories, to flush them away into the excess tide of unwanted experiences?

Dr. Anderson was the only person I could talk to about this, the only person who understood. He sounds like a silver trumpet, vibrant and bright.

Mom shouts a hurried "Get up" and leaves. I roll off the mattress and hit a wall. I'm not used to having my bed propped next to the right wall of my bedroom after years of having it on the left side. I'm half asleep and I thought I was still in

California. So this is what it's like to forget! Suddenly the day seems promising.

I pull on jeans and a clean T-shirt. My drawer is almost empty and Mom hasn't done laundry yet. I'm dangerously close to being forced to wear a large shirt I got years ago, a yellow SpongeBob atrocity. I'm not a math whiz, but I know that would exponentially lower my popularity index at Madison High School.

Mom is pouring herself a cup of coffee. A whiff of residue smoke tells me she's already been outside for a cigarette. Do I nag her so early in the morning? The kitchen is less cluttered; she unpacked some more boxes last night. The small, square table is cleared off, but the chairs still hold boxes marked "kitchen."

I smother my Cheerios in a cascade of milk and open three drawers to find the silverware. Then I move a box so I can sit at the table. Mom sets her cup down and moves a box so she can sit across from me.

"We need to do laundry," I say.

"Tomorrow. I promise. There's a Laundromat not too far away."

I smirk. "In Wellington, everything's not too far away."

"You should shower." Mom reaches over and runs her hand back and forth across my head, making even more of a knot of my dark curls.

"Can't. It's already 7:22. Don't have time," I say between mouthfuls.

"Someone is coming to hook up cable this afternoon. You'll be home, won't you?"

"Where else would I be?"

"I don't know. I thought you might want to join a sports team or something."

That came out of nowhere. I stop eating. "What kind of sport?"

"Any sport. Hockey? Basketball? It might be good for you."

"Are you joking? It's not like I'm going to become the next Wayne Gretzky just because we moved to Minnesota."

"How do you know if you don't try?"

"I can't skate and my ball skills are nonexistent. How's that for trying?"

Mom swirls her finger around the rim of her coffee cup. "I've never pushed you to do anything you didn't want to do, Baxter. I'm not that type of parent. Maybe I should have, though."

Her voice makes me stiffen. She doesn't play the guilt card often, but I can hear it coming out now.

She straightens up. "Did I tell you I used to play volleyball in high school? It's a good feeling to be part of a team, to work together toward a common goal. You could use that type of experience."

"I was in the Cub Scouts in California," I remind her. "For two years."

"Scouting isn't a sport."

"Okay, it's not volleyball, but there's definitely a competitive edge to getting that traffic safety badge."

That doesn't even get a small laugh. Mom purses her lips. "Okay, maybe something other than sports. Newspaper club or Debate. No, forget Debate. I don't know, Baxter. You spent the last few years cooped up at home except for the time you spent at the research center with Dr. Anderson and your tutor. Three years of watching old sitcoms on TV. But now you have a clean slate, a chance to start fresh. To do something different."

Her pity seeps across the table and into my bowl of cereal, making a soggy mess of the Cheerios. What she really means is that I have the chance to *be* something different. Someone besides who I am: the Memory Boy.

I put down my spoon. My stomach feels bloated, as though the cereal has expanded. Mom takes a small sip of her coffee. She's watching me, hoping for something that I can't give her. Her look makes me feel guilty. I ratted on her boyfriend and now she's moved us to northern Minnesota, the opposite end of the earth. She's left her friends and family and her job and Dink— well, he was the main reason we moved. But she did all that, mostly for me.

So I say what she wants to hear, even though it's difficult because I know it's a lie, and I have to grit my teeth to get it out before it escapes back inside.

"Okay." I force a half smile. "I'll find something. Maybe they have an art club." I figure it's the least I can offer after all she's done for me. Mom's always considered herself somewhat of an artist, so she'll love the idea of art club, if Madison High has such a thing. I can slop some paint on a piece of paper, even though I'm not artistic in the least.

Mom's face brightens. "I have a feeling this place is going to be great for both of us. Just don't forget—you're not the Memory Boy now."

I almost laugh. As if that was possible.

She remembers then. "Oh, right. You won't forget." But she sounds kind of sad when she says it.

I don't know what to say, so I go brush my teeth. The weight of the Cheerios presses in on me. Nothing scares me more than to see the hope in Mom's eyes.

Her voice is the same as it has always been: a breath of spring air, mixed with the scent of lilac that used to grow outside my bedroom window. It's the voice of promise.

As I stare at my reflection in the mirror, I wish I had an answer to that promise.

Freshman Orientation

Mom's optimism must have rubbed off. On my fourth day of school at Madison High I walk into the boys' bathroom, the one on the first floor, whistling the theme song from *The Andy Griffith Show*, and I'm completely blindsided by a hefty arm that squeezes my neck, pulling me into a headlock several inches above ground, leaving my feet dangling.

At first I think *Dink!* and I almost pee my pants. I don't want to die in the boys' bathroom. How did he find me so soon?

"New kid," a voice behind me belts out, "this is the *senior* bathroom."

Thank God it's not Dink. "How am I supposed to know that if I'm new?" I try to ask, but only a small gasp escapes.

"We're gonna have to help you *remember* so this doesn't happen again."

Good luck with that.

There's a swarm of them now, big football types, circling me. The bathroom is smoky, with a smell that's skunky but sweet at the same time. My face is tilted up toward the hazy fluorescent lights and the triangle-shaped tiles of the ceiling. Another guy moves into view. All I can see are black nose hairs and a pimply forehead. The beefy arm holds tight against my neck, preventing any movement and allowing very little breathing. But the voice behind me is twice-baked potatoes, warm and comforting. It's hard to believe that voice really wants to hurt me, even if the arms connected to that voice are wrapped around my neck. Of course, I'm a coward, so I don't fight back. I don't do anything except worry about my three-hundred-dollar atomic solar quartz watch. It was a gift from Dr. Anderson.

But the stress is too much. "Twice-baked," I squeak. The words come out before I can stop them.

"What? Did you just say 'twice-baked'?" The grip loosens.

I force out a small nod, not having much room to move my head.

"That's weird, dude."

"Maybe you're squeezing too hard and you stopped the blood flow to the brain," says the voice with nose hair, and he sounds like tar paper.

The grip loosens. I crash into the sink, gasping, rubbing my neck.

"Welcome to freshman orientation," Twice-baked says.

He shoves me and I land near the door. I use the opportunity to exit before tar-paper voice grabs me.

"Don't come back," they holler. Their laughter echoes in the hallway, an odd combination of tar and potatoes.

My watch! There's a scratch on the right side, probably from crashing into the sink. Why'd I go into that bathroom in the first place? Then I messed up by calling that kid "twice-baked." Dr. Anderson thinks that my synesthesia might have something to do with my unusual memory. Some people see numbers as colors, textures, or sounds. The number four could be green and pointy. I hear voices that way. But I don't tell people about it. I don't go up to girls and say, "Hey, did you know you sound like a shade of purple?" How would that affect my popularity index? Worse than wearing a SpongeBob T-shirt.

I'm six minutes late to Science. "Sorry," I murmur as I make my way to the back of the classroom. There's only one empty seat, and who's sitting across from me? None other than Halle Phillips. Even though my neck stings like rug burn, I'm out of breath, and sweat drips down my face from running up two flights of stairs, I decide that today is a good day. I wipe my forehead on my shirt sleeve.

Halle leans over and whispers, "It's not that hot out. Besides, I'd think you'd be used to the heat after living in California."

"Running. I overslept," I whisper between pants. That isn't technically a lie. I did oversleep. I was running.

"You weren't here yesterday," I add after I've caught my breath.

Her slim eyebrows shoot up. "Surprised you noticed. I switched from sixth period."

Mrs. Ball is calling for yesterday's homework. Halle passes hers up to the guy in front of her.

Crap. My backpack is on the bathroom floor three stories down. I'm not about to go back and get it. I think of the books and notebooks, the new pens and pencils, the calculator Mom bought me with an extended warranty. Will any of it still be there later?

I raise my hand. "I don't have my homework with me."

Mrs. Ball clicks her tongue. "You lose five points each day it's late." Double crap.

The rest of the class copy notes from the board. Halle hands me paper and a pencil.

"Thanks."

She nods like it's no big deal. She probably thinks I'm a slacker. First I need a tutor. Now I don't even have the basic supplies and my assignment is late.

It's hard to pay attention to Mrs. Ball the rest of the period with Halle sitting next to me. I steal glances at the pink stitching that runs down the sides of her jeans, the way a piece of hair sticks out of her brown barrette, and the way she squints when she's looking at the board. I pretend to take notes but watch her instead. Her handwriting is big and loopy and she makes little circles above her i's instead of dots.

After class, I duck and move in front of two other guys so I can walk out the door at the same time as her. Then I turn with her down the hallway, even though it's the opposite direction of my next class.

"Don't you hate Mrs. Ball?" Halle asks, as though it's perfectly natural for me to be there.

"Uh, I don't really know her."

"Consider yourself lucky. I've been badgering her for an

Environmental Science class for two years, even when I was in junior high. She says it doesn't fit into the curriculum. How crazy is that? We live in a town run by the taconite industry, our families are dying of mesothelioma, and our school doesn't care about environmental issues."

"Yeah, crazy," I agree. "At least your science books are newer. They were published in 1998."

She stops. "How do you know that? You don't even have yours with you."

I shouldn't have opened the book at all. Shouldn't have read a word of it. Then all this junk wouldn't be stuck in my head. I let out a nervous laugh. "I looked at it yesterday. Wanted to compare it to our books back in California."

"Oh. How do we compare?"

"Your books are newer."

"Well, there's that, I guess. But she still stinks as a teacher. Honestly, I could miss a whole year and just read the book and be ahead."

Funny, that's pretty much what I did for three years.

"What's mesothelioma?" I ask.

"It's a cancer caused by asbestos. My grandpa died of it last year. Lots of the mine workers here get it. It's found in taconite tailings, a waste product from extracting iron ore."

She stops in front of a classroom and lets out a small breath. "Thanks for listening to me rant. I'm done now. Promise. At least until next Science class. See you during homeroom."

I watch her disappear into the room and then I continue to stand at the door until the bell rings. That's how hopelessly, utterly mesmerized I am by her.

My next two classes are a blur. I don't even attempt to listen during World History. Instead I work on Mr. Shaw's assignment for Friday: to write down all the descriptions of Daisy Buchanan from the first three chapters of *The Great Gatsby*. My book is in my backpack somewhere on the third floor, but I don't need it. I borrow paper and pen and I write how Daisy had bright eyes and a bright passionate mouth, an excitement in her voice that men who had cared for her found difficult to forget. I write how she had a "lovely shaped face and a charming little laugh," the words Fitzgerald used to describe her. But the whole time I'm writing those words I'm thinking about Halle, of how they could apply to her. I wonder what Daisy Buchanan's voice would sound like, how it would compare to Halle's daffodil voice.

It's trouble to be spending so much time thinking about a girl who could potentially recognize me from Pascal Elementary. If I had a normal memory, would I have remembered her from kindergarten? Her righteous anger when I ragged on her imagination? The freckles around her nose that had faded slightly?

I like to think that I'd remember her regardless. But Halle can't possibly remember me. At least she left before I became known as the know-it-all kid who constantly corrected my teachers and challenged students to trivia contests. I was just trying to impress people the only way I knew how, with my memory. Throughout the three years Dr. Anderson spent studying me and performing memory tests on me, Mom wouldn't let him do any brain scans. After all that had happened, she said she just wanted to protect me. Or was she afraid of what he might find?

Most days I don't know what to hope for. A man named Solomon Shereshevskii who was born in 1886 had a near-perfect memory and synesthesia, too. He ended up working in a freak show performing feats of memory.

Personally, I'm hoping for something better than that.

My Plan to Win Halle

Not many guys get a second shot at love, so I intend to make the most of mine. The first thing I do is buy a bag of jelly beans. I only buy green ones because they're her favorite, or at least they were back in kindergarten. Then I talk Mom into buying me a yellow shirt, but I don't buy Big Bird yellow. I go with more of a straw color.

I place the bag of jelly beans in the middle of the library table before Halle arrives and lean back in the chair with my arms over the sides to show off my shirt. *Stay cool, suave, relaxed,* I tell myself. So I lean a bit more. Then I almost fall over backward.

My arms flail around in the attempt to catch myself. I can hear laughing and my face feels like I've just swallowed a hot pepper. This is one of those moments I wish I *could* forget. Then I see Halle standing next to me.

"What was that?"

"Impromptu workout." I twirl my arms. Stick out my chest under the yellow shirt.

"Right." She rolls her eyes. "Ooh, jelly beans. Can I have some?" She opens the bag and pops two in her mouth. "Green. My favorite!"

"They're my favorite, too," I say as I take a handful. Okay, that's not really true, but I do like them.

"Well, now that you've had your exercise, tell me what you know about the story." Halle's eyes fasten on mine like a clamp.

This is the hard part. I have to be careful not to spit back the book word for word, not to recite verbatim an entire chapter or a summary that sounds like something I got off Wikipedia. In the past teachers accused me of copying when I used the exact words, at least until they found out about my exceptional memory.

I stare down at *Gatsby* and try to pick my words carefully. A library helper walks by with a cart full of books. I read the titles as she passes. Two years from now I'll still remember them, be able to list them in alphabetical order. If I'd been born three hundred years ago, I could have been burned for witchcraft. If I'd been born eighty years ago, I could have been stuck in an insane asylum. Odd behavior begets odd punishment.

I should be doing math homework right now for my fifth-period class. My backpack was returned to me this morning after the janitor found it in the toilet in the first-floor bathroom. Miraculously, most of the contents weren't too wet. The calculator still works and my math book is readable, although the pages are curling at the bottom.

Halle crosses her arms and lets out a small sigh, as though I'm a hopeless case.

"Okay, let's try it another way. Do you think Nick is a reliable narrator? You have to remember that everything is filtered through his eyes."

"You mean do I believe everything he says?"

Halle nods.

"Yes and no. I mean, we have to look beyond what he says about himself and the other characters."

"So you don't trust him?"

"I guess I trust him to be true to his experience of the world. But he sees his own truth. We all see our own truth."

"What's the truth in these chapters?"

"Well, when he first sees Gatsby on the lawn, he's staring out at a green light across the sound and Nick thinks he sees him tremble. That green light promises something. Maybe hope or love, we don't know what yet. But we know that light and that action have some significance even if it is filtered through Nick's eyes."

"That's good, Baxter. Really good."

"Thanks," I say, relieved.

Then she crinkles her nose, what I've noticed she does when she doesn't understand something. "There's just one thing I can't figure out."

"What's that?"

She leans closer. "Now that we know the truth in *Gatsby*, tell me, what's the truth in Baxter Green?"

My jaw tightens and I press my thumb down hard on the book as I fight for control. "What do you mean?"

"I can tell you're smart. So why does Mr. Shaw want me to tutor you?"

"I got a C-minus on my first test."

"Yeah, but why did you get a C-minus? I took that same test. It was super easy."

The trouble with lies is that they don't hold up. It's like using a colander, trying to keep the truth from straining out with the watered-down lies. It always leaks through. Even Dink, who pitched lies more often than Mom smokes a cigarette, got caught.

I almost sound like Dink as I take the attack approach. "I'll tell you if you tell me why you sit in the back and don't wear your glasses when you can't see the board."

"How do you know I wear glasses?"

"You squint."

She stares at me long enough that I start feeling uncomfortable and I want to look away. But I don't. To look away would be backing down, admitting that I'm hiding something—which I am, but there's no way I'm admitting it.

Halle puts her elbow on the table and rests her chin in her hand. "Most guys would never have noticed that kind of stuff. Then there's the fact that we both like green jelly beans. It's so weird." She takes another handful from the bag.

I'm starting to sweat, but I fake a smile and raise one eyebrow. "I can't wait to find out what else we have in common." It's a cheesy thing to say. What I really want to tell her is that it's not weird, that there's a connection between us stretching back all the way to kindergarten and that you can fall in love when you're five, even if it's a different kind of love at that age, and that I notice everything about her; I always have. But that sounds even cheesier than what I said.

My comment brings a blush to her cheeks. But she recovers and smiles back at me and says something that takes me completely off guard. "So do you want to go to a protest rally after school?"

The funny thing is, she never said a word about my yellow shirt.

The Ragged Edge of the Universe

Even though I'm a firm believer in the truth, I can rationalize as well as the next guy. Mom said she wanted me to get involved in after-school activities. And okay, she probably didn't have this in mind. But Halle's eyes, the color of dark honey, definitely have something to do with my saying yes to a protest rally. I'd say yes to just about anything she asked me. And I get to spend more time with her. I get to be with her outside of school.

I know it doesn't mean she likes me. But she wouldn't have asked me if she thought I was a loser. Or would she? Is this her new-kid pity duty?

My only problem is how I'll answer Mom's questions without lying when I get home. That's another rationalization, one I'll think about later.

We meet in the parking lot after school, near a black

rusted-out van with more metal showing than paint. But what makes the van stand out in the sea of cars are the environmental bumper stickers plastered around the sides: GO GREEN, SAVE THE ENVIRONMENT; KEEP THE PLANET CLEAN, IT'S NOT URANUS; REDUCE, REUSE, RECYCLE. There are funny ones, too: IF BARBIE IS SO POPULAR, WHY DO YOU HAVE TO BUY HER FRIENDS? and MY OTHER CAR IS A PIECE OF SHIT. A slew of Vikings decals fill the spots between the stickers, giving a purple haze to the black metallic spaces that are left open.

I arrive at 2:43. Halle introduces me to the group. I file away their descriptions in my mind: Gina, who has dark hair and pale skin and is in my study hall; and Roxie, who's built like a linebacker, with a pretty face, long blond hair, and a butterfly tattoo on her upper arm. The driver of the van is an upperclassman.

"This is Eddie," Halle says. "Our fearless leader."

Eddie smirks. "That's because I'm the only one with a driver's license." His long black hair sweeps down past his shoulders. He has dark, intense eyes, and a T-shirt with a turtle on it. I think about commenting but decide against it. I don't know how sensitive this guy is and he has thirty pounds on me. He can definitely whip my ass.

I hold out my hand. Eddie just nods. "Welcome to the Environmental Club. You ever been arrested?"

I let out a short gasp.

Eddie's face breaks into a wide grin. "Had you going, didn't I?"

Halle nudges me into the van. "You really look worried, New Kid. You have a police record or something?"

How'd she know? "I have a mom who'd freak out if I got arrested." But I'm way more worried about a paper trail for Dink to follow. Worse than that would be my picture splattered across CNN.

"Don't worry. We're law-abiding, peaceful protesters."

"And we're related to people who work in the mines and processing plants," Gina adds. She sits next to Eddie in the front. He puts his arm around her. Halle sits in the far back with Roxie, which leaves me alone in the middle seat.

Handmade posters and flyers litter the floor, along with empty soda cans and wrappers. Eddie has eaten at every fast food chain in town and most of it is ground into the dirty gray carpet.

"You're protesting where your families work?"

"It's okay," Halle says. "Our parents can't get fired just because of their activist-minded children."

I briefly wonder if there's any inherent danger of Mom losing her job at the Tin Cup, but if they aren't worried about their parents, then I shouldn't be, either.

Eddie makes a wide turn and the contents of the floor shift left. "But people don't support us," he says. "The Wellington Mine Company employs ninety percent of the people who live here. The town would disappear without it."

"So why protest?"

Roxie's soft voice drifts from behind me. "Because I want my parents to be safe. They breathe in taconite powder every day at work." She sounds like dandelion fluff.

"What kind of music you like, Baxter?"

"I'm good with whatever," I reply. I don't listen to music

because it gets tied in to the memory of when I heard it, each and every time.

"For the new guy, here's an Iron Range song. It's the only song I like from my parents' generation." Eddie pushes a button and the sounds of "Endless Highway" fill the van. I expected heavy metal music from Eddie. His voice is a boulder.

Halle leans forward, her elbows on the back of my seat. She whispers in my ear. It tickles and I hunch my shoulders. "Bob Dylan grew up on the Range. All the old people listen to him here."

Eddie drives slowly, or maybe the van isn't capable of going any faster than thirty miles an hour. He turns and pulls up to a drive-through lane. Fumes from the exhaust leak in the windows. I hold my breath.

Eddie leans out the window. "Who wants a burger?"

Everyone yells their order at the same time. I end up with a burger and Coke I didn't order, but I pay for and eat it anyway.

Halle orders fries. "I'm a vegetarian, but I'm not that strict. I don't mind a little meat grease in my fries."

We drive past a lake and head north of town. It's 3:30. I know I'm supposed to be at home waiting for the cable guy, and I can't say what every other teen says when he blows off something his mom told him to do. I can't say I forgot.

When I was little, Mom accidentally closed the car door on my pinkie. Just thinking about it makes my eyes water and my finger throb. I used to think that's how everyone's memory worked, that you're trapped in those memories, and every hurtful experience and bad choice is with you forever.

So I'm worried that I'm making a bad choice now; ditching the cable guy to ride in a beat-up van and protest in front of a taconite plant. We drive past scattered buildings and farms, and soon those fade away, too. Steep banks give way to pine trees, small lakes, and wide canyons filled with gray-and-red rock, all of it man-made. A line from *Gatsby* plays in my head about the Midwest being the ragged edge of the universe. If that's true, then the Iron Range is the pit at the bottom of that edge.

There's a feeling of desolation and destruction out here. Halle calls it the rape of the land. The buildings of Wellington Mines rise up from a cloud of red dust in the distance like a lost city. A huge lost city. Warehouse-sized buildings and trucks that dwarf Eddie's van are surrounded by tall chain-link fences. I feel as though we've entered another world.

Eddie parks the van in weeds next to the road just outside the entrance.

"Aren't we going inside?" I ask.

Eddie shakes his head and reaches back for one of the home-made signs. "Not allowed inside the fence. But we'll catch the four o'clock shift change."

Everyone grabs a sign and tumbles out of the van. I pick up what's left: a bent piece of yellow cardboard with a paint stick fastened to the bottom. It has black printed letters on it that read, TACONITE KILLS!

"I'm getting better signs made," Halle says. "Professional quality. Ones that will blow them away."

Her sign is white with computer-printed letters on it: KEEP OUR WORKERS SAFE.

"And better slogans. Catchier phrases."

"How long have you been doing this?" I ask.

"Would you believe this is just our second demonstration? We formed the club in junior high at the end of last year. It was just Gina and Roxie and me. This year we tried it at the high school. Seven kids showed up at our first meeting, but two left and never returned. And then my ex quit as soon as we stopped dating. So now it's just the four of us, five counting you, if we don't scare you away. Gina says we should change our name to the 'Mental Club.'"

"Is this what you usually do at your meetings?"

She smiles at me like I'm a little kid. " 'Course not. We usually scale corporate smokestacks to hang our protest banners and row out in rubber rafts to save baby seals."

A few seconds pass before I respond. "Oh. That was a joke."

"So you could at least pretend to laugh!"

"I would have, but . . ."

"What?"

"I almost believed you."

She laughs. The daffodils shimmer in her voice, as though someone plucked them and is twirling them around a finger. "My reputation precedes me."

"I've heard rumors," I confess.

Halle turns and shouts behind her as she's walking. "They're not rumors, New Kid. Completely true."

Halle has on a red short-sleeved jacket over a black skirt, and short black boots that show off her long legs. She looks out of place with the rest of us, who wear jeans and T-shirts. She looks out of place on a dusty road in front of a factory. She should be in a fashion magazine.

A memory of Halle pops into my head. It was the first time we learned about endangered species.

On September 18, our kindergarten teacher, Mrs. Skrove, read us a story about California condors and told us how they soar on wind currents instead of flapping their wings, about how they were sacred to the Native Americans, and how at one point there were less than twenty-five of them left in the wild. Then we colored pictures of condors and a week later we saw one at the zoo during a class field trip. Halle colored her condor a bright yellow, but the one at the zoo was black and white with a pinkish head.

"He looks ugly," she said.

I thought he looked awesome. I bought a stuffed animal condor from the gift shop. Halle bought a tiger but later said she wished she had a condor, too.

"Even though he's ugly, I don't want him to extinct," she said. "I just wish he was yellow."

I still have my stuffed animal condor. I wonder if she still has her tiger. I follow Halle to the gate, where Eddie and the two girls are standing with the signs pointed down, waiting for traffic.

The air smells different here, like the fillings the dentist uses in teeth—hot metal. A swirl of white rises above the plant, then floats into a nearby cloud.

Roxie follows the swirl with her eyes. "Do you remember how in fifth grade we each got a package of taconite pellets during Minnesota history month? How we played marbles with them?"

Eddie laughs. "I remember that. The pellets made good slingshot ammo, too. You ever see them set off charges in the field?

You could be half a mile away, watching them blast a cloud of clay and dust a hundred feet in the air, and still come home covered in dust."

"My family was involved in mining before the taconite plants," Halle says. "Grandpa said it was in our blood. Of course, he died because it was in his lungs."

Gina squints up at the sun. "Would you all stop? This is *sooo* depressing. What time is it? I have to babysit my brothers at five-thirty."

I look at my watch. "Three twenty-seven." What will Mom say when she gets home and the cable isn't hooked up?

Gina points at my watch. "How can you tell time with that thing? It's got more dials than the cockpit of an airplane." Funny she should say that. She sounds like a landing strip.

"My do— my friend gave it to me." Shoot. I almost said doctor.

"Do you have to watch *all* your brothers?" Halle asks Gina.

Gina nods. "Stop over later and help me. Please, oh, please? I'll pay you half."

"No thanks. Last time I helped you, all four of them dog-piled on top of me. Going to your house makes me happy I only have one older sister."

"Here comes a car!" Roxie holds up her sign and the rest of us follow her lead.

The driver stares but doesn't acknowledge us as he turns off the highway and passes through the gate. It's as though we're part of the landscape; an unwanted shrub or an odd-shaped rock.

"Jerk," Eddie yells after him.

Halle jabs Eddie with her sign. "Point of order, Mr. President. We're not here to harass people."

"Yeah, well, I know that guy. He *is* a jerk."

Eight more cars pass by. The reactions are all the same. We're evidently not wanted here.

"They could at least honk their horns in support," Gina complains.

"Or nod," Roxie says. "Or make eye contact."

"Why would it be any different than last time?" Eddie says. "They're all idiots."

"We knew this wasn't going to be easy," Halle says. "But the whole point of our club is to stand up for what we believe, even if it isn't a popular opinion."

"It takes time to convince people to do the right thing," Roxie adds.

"It shouldn't," Eddie replies. "People are dying in this town. Do the right thing. End of discussion."

He steps out onto the road and stabs his sign at the next car that goes past. The driver swerves around him and honks.

"Yeah, that's what I'm talking about. Notice us, you asshole!"

Gina rubs his shoulder. "Calm down, baby. We don't want to get in trouble."

Eddie sounds so angry. What if he goes ballistic? His earlier question haunts me; we actually *could* get arrested.

But maybe he's like the sound of his voice, a large boulder that has to make a splash.

I try not to pigeonhole people. But it's confusing when a person's voice doesn't match his personality. I knew a kid at my old school who sounded like sharp needles. I couldn't stand being around him. He might have been a good kid once I got to know him, but I never gave him a chance. It irritated my ears just listening to him.

Halle steps out in front. "Let's focus here. We're making a statement, regardless of how they react. We can't expect to change the world in one day." Listening to her is soothing and exhilarating at the same time.

We're standing in the road, not blocking traffic exactly, but definitely out there when another car drives up, a black Cadillac with tinted windows.

"Uh-oh. Management," Roxie murmurs.

The car slows down and stops next to our group. At this point I'm tempted to drop my sign and run off into the ditch. The only thing that's stopping me is Halle. She would probably think I'm weak and gutless. I stand behind Eddie and peek around him.

The darkened window rolls down and everyone backs away except for Halle. She approaches the car. Her bravery makes me feel like a spineless slug. But her daffodil voice breaks slightly when she speaks.

"Hello, Daddy."

Embracing the Green Light

"But we're not doing anything wrong!" Halle's voice bounces off the hot pavement and carries back to the rest of us huddled near the side of the road.

"I'm going over there," Eddie says. He throws down his sign.

"No." Gina pulls him back. "It's *her* dad."

We inch closer. I can't make out Mr. Phillips's voice, but Halle's shoulders droop and her face is flushed when she turns back to look at us.

"We're not holding up a sign advertising who I am," she says hotly and points at us. "They all have relatives here. The whole town does!"

Gina takes a step back. "Why'd she have to say that?"

Finally, the car pulls away. Halle turns and straightens herself. "We have to go," she says in a flat voice. "Now." Eddie doesn't object. He takes one look at Halle's face and puts down his sign as though his anger has disintegrated into the warm pavement.

The mood in the van is church quiet. The signs rest in a pile at my feet on top of a half-eaten container of fries. Eddie's mumbling something to Gina, but I can't hear him over the noise of the engine.

It's selfish to be thinking of myself now, but I can't help it. I'm relieved we weren't arrested and that Eddie didn't do anything rash like throw his sign at the Cadillac. The only person in trouble is Halle. She said her dad worked at Wellington Mines. But management? From the looks of that Cadillac, he's in *upper* management.

I have a fantasy relationship with my own father. In my mind he takes me fishing even though Mom doesn't remember him ever doing that. It's that Andy Griffith thing. He brags about me and protects me and he can kick Dink's butt. Of course this fantasy keeps me from seeing him as human with flaws, of which Mom assures me he had plenty. And it keeps me from understanding how Halle can be so rebellious toward her father.

But I want to understand. I turn around. Halle is staring straight ahead like she's in a coma. I'm surprised she hasn't stared a hole into the headrest in front of her. "So, that was your dad?" I ask her.

Roxie rolls her eyes.

Halle answers without turning her gaze. "Yes. The big bad wolf is Daddy." She looks at me and her eyes are defiant. "Now you know the truth about Halle Phillips. She's a fake."

"No you're not," Roxie objects. "You can't help what your father does."

"But I live with the enemy. I should give back every stitch of clothing he ever bought me, and the dance lessons, and the flute. I should live on the streets instead of living with him."

Seems a bit drastic, but then again, we moved to Minnesota to get away from Dink. Though I doubt that her dad is the same rank of enemy as Dink.

"You don't have to move out to be yourself," Roxie says. "Just be true to your beliefs."

"And tell your old man we're not giving up," Eddie shouts from the front. "We'll be back."

"Yeah," Gina says. "He can't stop you from protesting. It's your right and your duty. Stand tall and brave, girl."

I want to say something encouraging to let her know I understand how she feels. But the truth is that I *don't* understand. Being true to myself has never been an aspiration of mine. I yearn to be someone different, so that ten years from now Dink will be a faint memory and the past won't be a constant intrusion.

"What about you, Baxter?" Halle's eyes flash a challenge, but I'm not sure what that challenge means. Is she asking me to be part of this group? Or does she want to know how I feel about her situation?

Would Halle be saying this if she knew who I was? I feel guilty because there isn't anyone who's more of a fake than me. I work hard at being a fake. And today it actually helped. For a few hours, Dink has retreated from my mind. So have the intruding memories. That alone is significant. Maybe this is what Dr. Anderson meant when he said that leading a full life can help curb the isolation I feel. This is the first time in a long time that I've felt part of something. Even if it is the Mental Club.

My reinvented self hesitates but the truth forces its way out. I moved here to find a lost love and a new life. Like Gatsby, I believe in that green light.

"Count me in."

The Art of Lying to Your Mom

"So unlike you, Baxter. You could have at least called." Mom is digging through a box of odds and ends. She's looking for an ashtray, an openly symbolic piece of ceramic that I made in second grade before I was anti-smoking. Her voice isn't angry, though. She seems almost pleased that I screwed up.

"Sorry. The meeting lasted longer than I expected. I got home at 4:55; before you, but after the cable guy."

"Well, next time . . ." She doesn't finish. Maybe saying it out loud will jinx it. I've found a place to go that isn't a research facility and people to hang out with who don't wear white lab coats. To her, it's a sign of a normal teen life.

She stands and gives up on the box. "Don't get me wrong, I'm glad you took our talk this morning to heart. But the Environmental Club? What made you choose that?"

A pair of brown eyes. Here's the part where I have to lie.

There's no way around it, I've decided, so I've been rehearsing since I got home. The key is to keep my voice even so Mom buys it. I repeat part of a lecture I heard while flipping through the channels on TV last year. "The impact of environmental choices affects us all. More than thirty-eight species of dragon-flies have been identified in northern Minnesota. They have very specific habitat requirements, and disturbances in those habitats from water pollution, changes in shoreline vegetation, or changes in forest cover may cause them to disappear."

Mom frowns. "I didn't know you were into dragonflies."

"Neither did I. I'm trying something new."

"Hmm. I guess I can't complain. But how did you get home? You must have missed the bus."

"Eddie gave me a ride. He's a senior and the president of the club."

"Oh, maybe next time I can meet him." There it is again. Her voice fills the room with promise.

"I also got offered a job," I tell her. "Just a few afternoons and weekends helping bale hay."

Mom's eyes widen. "You know how to bale hay?"

"No. But how hard can it be? I need some money of my own to spend." And I've decided that Brad is right. Halle's not going to be won over by a few green jelly beans.

"What about schoolwork? What about the C-minus?"

"Not a problem. I can handle it."

She twists her mouth sideways and makes a weird face. It's her thinking pose. "I suppose. But you'll have to find a ride and if your grades don't go up you'll have to quit."

"I can ride there with Brad after school a couple days each week if you can pick me up later. And it's just a temporary job."

"Are you sure you're my son? This morning you didn't want to do anything, and in one day you've joined a club and you have a part-time job." She shakes her head in disbelief. "Well, I guess it will be good for you. All this fresh, North-Country air." Then she goes outside to have a cigarette. She doesn't even see the irony in it.

It strikes me when she leaves; how easy it was to lie to her. I've avoided telling lies my whole life, felt that it was against my nature. I imagined my tongue bursting into flames like a vampire caught in bright sunlight. But I'm standing here without any burns or gashes and only a tiny bit of guilt to bother me. Nothing I can't handle.

Lies are easier than secrets. No one forgets a secret, not even people with average memories. Secrets are heavy. They're anchors that weigh a person down; the longer you keep them the heavier they become. And that thought sends me to my closet once again to check out my guitar case. I gave the guitar to the Salvation Army years ago.

"You're gonna love this," Dink said. "I always wanted one when I was a kid." He took the guitar out of the case and tuned the strings as he held the pick on the end of his tongue. Then he strummed a few chords and belted out a horrible rendition of Willie Nelson's "On The Road Again."

I was eleven years old and couldn't have cared less about a guitar. It was an expensive one, with a solid spruce top. It was a bribe; a week later he asked me to help him at work.

But what irked me was the fact that he bought me something that I had absolutely no interest in. Dink didn't bother to find out what I'd like, even for a bribe.

I run my hand through the money, thinking about Dink's scam. It wasn't anywhere near as good as the scam he pulled on Mom. He got her to fall for him, to want a future with him, to let him live with us. There isn't near-enough money here to make up for what he did.

How I Become a Stalker

It's 8:50 and Halle hasn't shown up for school yet. I'm consumed with worry because I don't know anything about her dad. What if he transferred her to another school or locked her in her room?

The events from yesterday replay in my head: the darkened windows of the car as it pulled up next to us, the sound of Halle's voice as she spoke to her father. But nothing gives me a clue as to where Halle is today.

When Mr. Feege asks if anyone remembers the sample math problem he posted on the board yesterday, I'm so preoccupied with Halle that I raise my hand and recite it verbatim. Everyone stares, including Mr. Feege. He'd used a calculator to get the answer yesterday.

"I wrote it down," I say, pointing at my notebook. Luckily,

no one notices that it's just scribbled writing, most of which is Halle's name in various fonts.

At 10:57 I catch Roxie in the hall between classes. "Halle wasn't in class. Have you seen her?"

She shakes her head. "She's not at school. I haven't talked to her since yesterday."

Roxie notices the frown on my face. "I'm sure it's nothing," she says in a whispery voice. "Halle cuts class sometimes."

But when Halle doesn't show for our tutoring session, I can't shake the feeling that something's wrong. I use one of the computers and search the local white pages for Phillips. There are two listed in Wellington: one near downtown, and another on the outskirts. Both are about two miles from my house.

I write down the addresses and wait until Mrs. Algren is finished talking to another student before I approach her. She has curly, dark hair and kind eyes that light up whenever someone walks into the library. I show her the paper with my writing on it.

"Mrs. Algren, at which address would a wealthy owner most likely live in Wellington?"

Her eyebrows shoot up. "Is this your roundabout way of asking me where Halle Phillips lives?"

My neck flushes hot. Even if I tried to lie about this, she'd know.

She nods. "Thought so. Her older sister used to belong to our book club and I gave her a ride home a few times. She lives on Willow Way, the second address."

"Thanks."

"If you see her, tell her I just got in a new book she'd enjoy."

"I will." And like that, my mind is made up. When I get off the bus at 3:02, I turn in the opposite direction of our house. There's a crisp breeze in the air that makes my nose run. Leaves are falling from trees, littering yards and sidewalks and clogging up gutters.

I follow the street signs, walking down Illinois Avenue. My memory is nonselective, a human Xerox machine as I pass through neighborhoods. *House number 1492, a gray rambler with white trim. A red Chevy van in the driveway, Minnesota license number XHA 418.*

I avert my eyes and stare down at the pavement. Dr. Anderson said I need to make a conscious effort *not* to notice things; that way I won't remember them. But it's hard. I can't help noticing. It's the way my brain has always worked.

Most people think it's strange to have a memory like mine. But it's just as strange to me when someone can't remember where she placed her car keys fifteen minutes earlier or what assignment the teacher gave us two days ago.

After crossing the railroad tracks I stop at a convenience store. The shriveled hot dogs smell good and I'm tempted to buy one, but then I notice the grime on the rack beneath them. A burly man picks one off the rack and I see that same grime on the underside of the hot dog. So I buy a Gatorade and guzzle it, then make my way up a hill toward the outskirts of Wellington. Each step brings me closer to Willow Way and also closer to a panic-induced stomachache.

How will Halle feel about me looking up her address and coming to her house? Will she think I'm stalking her? I realize

I have no idea how she'll react. The uncertainty slows my footsteps. Maybe I should turn around and go home. Maybe I should call her first.

I look up at the street sign in front of me. Willow Way. I turn and follow the narrow, curvy road of spacious brick homes that are three times the size of our townhome. They sweep out and down across a rolling hill. I've seen big homes before, but not in this town. Are all of them owned by executives at the plant?

At 3:50 I stand in front of Halle's house. One word describes it: colossal. It has turrets on each side and rounded windows. The lawn is meticulously landscaped with maple trees and bushes with satiny leaves that look as though they've been polished, unlike our house, which has an ash tree in front and a single rosebush in the back. A rounded driveway leads to the house, which backs up to a small lake. Behind her house I see a distant dock extending out from the sloping shoreline.

She's so out of my league. But even though I know it's true, I don't want to blow my shot at her, even if it's a slim shot at best. Part of me wants to leave. The other part insists on staying to find out if Halle is okay. On the side of the house are huge ground-floor windows, ones that I might see into if I walk past. Maybe I can get a glimpse of Halle and I won't have to knock on her door and come up with an explanation as to why I'm here.

My shoes leave footprints in the short grass. I try to look casual, not like a Peeping Tom, which is what I feel like. Knee-high bushes frame the windows. In between is a planting of flowers. I sneak around the edge of the bushes. My heart pounds with the thought of catching a glimpse of her, like a breath of air to hold me until tomorrow. My inner critic goes into overdrive: this is dangerous, maybe even creepy. But I don't feel like a pervert; I feel like a concerned friend. The driving force that brought me here is the result of eleven years of remembering Halle, of missing her in my life. I just have to know she's okay.

I pass two windows that are covered by blinds. I peek around the corner of the third window into a room that radiates opulence with its mahogany furniture and stone-carved fireplace. As luck would have it, Halle is there, sitting on an oversized chair. Her head is down and she's reading something. I can't tell what.

"Halle," a voice calls. She looks up.

"In here."

A man enters the room. His eyes are bright like Halle's, but they hold more intensity.

"I'm leaving for a meeting. Don't forget to load the dishwasher." His voice is condescending, like she's ten instead of fifteen. He sounds like hot furnace air, and his voice crowds the room.

"I'm not going to stop protesting. Neither are my friends."

"You don't tell me what you're going to do, young lady."

"He was my grandpa," she yells, and there are tears in her voice. "He was your dad. How can you not care?"

Her father shakes his head and rubs his forehead. "I don't have time for this." He turns and leaves.

Her shoulders are shaking. She throws her book down. It's *Gatsby*.

The garage door opens. I turn and catch my right foot on the bush. My body flies back onto the flowers, flattening them. "Ouch!"

Then I hear movement inside. I crawl toward the bush, away from the window. Halle's father backs the Cadillac out into the curved driveway and heads down the street.

I limp out into the street. I hope Halle's tear-filled eyes didn't see me. Her dad is a jerk for making her cry and acting like her opinion doesn't matter. And I know all about jerks.

"Come here, Baxter," Dink called me over. He'd just moved in the week before. I still didn't know him all that well, but I knew I was starting to annoy him because he spent most of his time in his office with the door closed.

"What is it?"

I stood in front of him and he pulled up his shirt sleeve to show me his tattooed bicep: a blue gargoyle with red eyes and devil horns surrounded by orange flames.

Dink flexed his arm. The gargoyle's mouth opened wide, as if it were going to eat me.

"Gross!" I ran and hid under my bed. I could hear Dink's laughter in his office, his muddy water voice splashing across the carpet. I stayed under my bed until Mom got home from work.

I push up my coat sleeve and focus on my watch. The dials turn around and around and the memory eases.

I didn't always have this problem. The memories started intruding the week after I testified against Dink. They were vivid and sporadic, slamming me in the chest when I least expected. Maybe it was timing, Dr. Anderson had said. A certain age. But I knew it was Dink.

The street narrows at the corner and I hobble down Willow Way, favoring my left foot. I can't get rid of my own memories, but I can find something nice to do for Halle—something to make those tears a faded memory, at least for her.

Why I Don't Understand Women

I'm lying on my bed reading *The Great Gatsby* when I hear Mom's muffled voice in the next room. She's talking to Aunt Val. Mom's voice always changes when she's talking on the phone to her sister. She says that it's because Aunt Val makes her feel like the little sister when they talk.

Later, when I go to get a soda, Mom is sitting on the kitchen floor, organizing the pans on the bottom shelf. Her eyes are red and blotchy.

"How's Aunt Val?"

Mom immediately wipes her eyes. "How did you know I was talking to her?"

"You talk to her every day."

"She's fine. She's just found out that she's going to be a grandma." Mom flashes a sad smile as she moves the pans around.

Why does that make Mom sad? Is it the thought that she might never have grandchildren? Does she think I'll never have a relationship or get married or have kids? Or is it because she's getting too old to have kids of her own?

I open the fridge. "Wow. Justin and Trista. That's great."

"Yeah." She pauses. "She also said that Dink called her."

My hand freezes on the can of soda. I can feel my heart pounding in my chest. "Dink?"

"She didn't tell him anything. He was Mr. Personality. You know how he can be. Said he still loves me, that he misses us."

Missed his money was more like it. My voice breaks. "You sure she didn't tell him anything?"

"No, she promised she wouldn't. We're safe, Baxter. You don't have to worry."

Dink called Aunt Val. That means he's looking for us, that everything I feared is true. I can almost feel his slimy breath on my neck.

The linoleum creaks beneath my feet. I'm clenching my soda and staring at Mom, until it hits me. She's crying over Dink. How could she cry for that guy?

February 23, at 7:37. Their first date. Dink handed the dozen roses to Mom. "Beautiful flowers for a beautiful woman."

She blushed. "They're gorgeous. You shouldn't have, but I'm glad you did." They both laughed, but Dink's laugh sounded forced.

Another memory flashes: *July 18, at 10:44 p.m. Dink had another dozen roses in his hands. He was in the kitchen. Mom had just come home from her job at the newspaper. From the living room I could only see part of her, one hand on her hip. Dink's voice was*

*pleading. "Come on, Mary. You know I work on commission. Things
are tough right now. I'll help out as soon as I can."*

*"Why do you spend money on flowers when you can't help with the
rent? You've only paid me one time in the last eight months,"* she hissed
in a low voice. *Mom didn't like to fight in front of me. She knew I'd
remember it.*

"I have expenses, too," he said angrily. *"I pull my weight around
here. Who fixed that leaky faucet last week? You're lucky to have me."*

*He threw the roses against the wall. Red petals scattered across the
floor. Then he slammed the back door on his way out. I knew he'd come
home drunk. He always did when they fought.*

I wonder which memory Mom's thinking of as she cries
now. I go back to my room and *Gatsby*, and I read how Daisy's
husband Tom broke his girlfriend's nose with his open hand
in a single instant.

Dink's temper was like that. Unpredictable. One minute he
was acting like we were best buddies, the next he was yelling
at me and trying to scare me into doing what he wanted.

I didn't steal Dink's money because he'd slapped me that
one time. I stole Dink's money because he used Mom and
me. He made us trust him, and then he made me write down
those credit card numbers. He was a fake from the start, and
we both fell for it.

Thoughts of Dink creep into my bed, making it impossible
to sleep. Every sound unnerves me. Rattling windows. Creaking walls. The sound of a car driving by. Distant footsteps.

"I know what you did, Baxter." Dink's voice reached across the
aisle of the courtroom. *"You took my money, didn't you?"*

"Don't listen to him. He's going to prison. You don't have to see him ever again," Mom said, taking me in her arms.

"Give it back," Dink shouted. "I know you have it!"

The guards pulled him away. Mom started crying. I pretended I didn't hear Dink, but I could see him through the crease in Mom's sweater. He was swearing and tugging against the guards like a dog on a leash.

What will happen if Dink finds us? Why didn't Mom kick him out sooner? Why did Daisy stay with her cheating husband when she had someone like Gatsby who adored her?

I turn on the light and continue reading, rooting for Gatsby to win in the end as if my own life depends on it.

My First Date

On the way to school I sit in my usual spot on the bus, fifth seat from the front on the left-hand side. We're halfway to school when a green car passes us going in the opposite direction. For a moment I think it's a Camaro. A metallic, fern green Camaro. But I'm not sure because I only got a glimpse and it's gone now.

I lean my head against the window and clutch my stomach. I have an acid taste in my throat. I look at my watch but the memories spill out like a waking dream and I'm stuck back with him again.

I wrote the numbers down. Dink grabbed the paper from my hand.

"I wish I could take you to Vegas, Baxter. Maybe when you're a little older." He sounded all friendly, like he hadn't just slapped me across the face twenty minutes ago, like we were buddies again. But I wouldn't forget. I'd never forget.

Just the thought of Dink makes me sick. That acid taste fills my whole mouth. I imagine last night's chicken splattering across the bus floor and I open the window and gulp air.

An hour later I'm staring down at my Social Studies book, trying to get the memory of Dink out of my head when two hands reach around and cover my eyes.

"Did you miss me?" Halle's bubbly, daffodil voice provides instant relief. My stomach is no longer queasy and everything is okay, even the fact that I'm a Peeping Tom and totally unworthy of her.

She reminds me of Daisy at that moment, so I respond the way Fitzgerald would have written it in *Gatsby*. "The whole school is desolate. They were planning to paint their notebooks black until you returned."

She removes her hand. My skin tingles at the memory of her touch.

Halle scrunches up her nose. "You're kind of odd sometimes, Baxter."

I flash a blank look back. Did she see me peeking in her window yesterday?

Then her eyes turn playful. "Want to go out to lunch with me?"

"We have different lunch periods. I have second and you have third."

"And your point is?"

"You want me to . . . ?"

"Skip." The word rolls off her tongue like a challenge.

I let out a nervous laugh.

"Don't tell me you've never skipped before."

I think back to my days with Coyote. A private tutor is best left unmentioned. "I was homeschooled for the last three years," I say instead. "It's hard to skip there."

She shakes her head. "See what you've missed? It's absolutely expected in high school. What classes do you have after lunch?"

"Phys Ed and Lit."

Mrs. Ball makes a shushing sound as she writes on the board. Halle sits down and murmurs, "Everyone skips Phys Ed. And you can definitely skip Shaw's class. Meet me in the south parking lot at twelve-thirty."

Like a gypsy who's satisfied with the spell she's cast, Halle opens her book and doesn't so much as glance my way the rest of the period. I spend the entire morning in a nervous rush, weighing the consequences of skipping. But the debate going on in my head isn't a fair one. I'm going to skip; I can't deny the pull Halle has on me. If it was anyone but her I wouldn't do it. I'm too much of a wimp.

But there are other things to consider. Mom, if she finds out. My teachers, who already think I'm a slacker because I barely take notes, and even though I'm getting better grades, I'm still careful not to ace my quizzes. And there's the concern that Halle and her friends are a bit on the extreme side. Eddie seems like a hothead, and if Halle really smashed in a pop machine in junior high, what's to say that smashing down a taconite-plant fence won't soon follow? I was released by the police because I ratted out Dink and I was only twelve years old. But I don't need unnecessary attention.

At 12:28 I stand outside the door and lean against a brick

wall warmed by the sun, trying to look like I'm waiting for a ride, like I'm supposed to be here. I've never cut class before, and never had a girl invite me to lunch, either. Two firsts. I'm not sure how to act. Is this a date? Should I pay? I only have ten dollars on me.

Halle bursts out the door with a bright smile on her face, as if skipping school is the best thing in the world. She looks at me and clicks her tongue. "If it will make you feel better, we'll talk about *Gatsby* during lunch. Then you won't feel so guilty."

"Is it that obvious?"

"Completely," she says and her voice sparks of glee. "Come on." She pulls me up a grassy hill toward a street leading downtown. I don't know where we're going but I don't really care. *Carefree.* The word flits through my mind, making a new connection.

"Were you sick yesterday?" I ask.

She shakes her head. "Sick, tired, burned out. I know; it's only the second week of school."

"Why do you hate school so much?"

"I don't hate it. I'm just not all that into it. When I was a little girl I was so excited to go to kindergarten. I thought it was going to be this great adventure I'd heard my sister talk about. So finally the first day of school came. I went and met my teacher and the other kids; I remember we had this huge castle in our classroom that I loved."

"Made out of gray cardboard." The words fly out of my mouth before I can stop them.

"Yeah. How did you know?"

"I . . . I've seen one before."

"God, Baxter. You're always one step ahead of me. Well, anyway, after I got home, my mom asked how it was and I said, 'Just okay,' because no one played with me in the castle, and Mom said, 'Well, you'll have more fun tomorrow.' And I said, 'You mean I have to go back?' I thought it was a one-shot deal. I had no idea that school went on for twelve long years."

That first day of kindergarten Halle wore a red jumper with a white polo top and white knee socks. The first time I saw her she was inside the castle, peeking out through the bookmark-sized openings at the rest of the class, singing a little song to herself about a teapot. I liked her the minute I heard her voice. Then I saw her cherub face and curly blond pigtails and I was hopelessly in love. But she was very shy; she kept hiding inside the castle whenever I looked at her, so I didn't talk to her that day. Instead I played an alphabet matching memory game with Danny Jamison. Danny was horrible at it.

Halle sighs. "Mom broke it to me gradually. Kept telling me I had a few more days. Then I eventually figured it out on my own. But school is so boring. If it weren't for Shaw's class I wouldn't show up at all."

We walk down the tree-lined streets of Wellington. The homes are older, not as big as Halle's, but they're what Mom calls quaint. She says they each have a character and a history. I'd never thought of houses that way.

Our shoes crunch leaves that are falling off trees even though it's warm enough to wear shorts. The trees seem to know that autumn is here even if the weather doesn't. "So I take it you're not interested in college?"

"No, but I don't have a choice. It's expected. The problem is I'm too smart for school. It's not challenging."

"You could take advanced classes."

"Did I mention that I'm also lazy? And I love to watch daytime soaps on TV?"

"It gets lonely studying by yourself. I did it for three years."

"Well, I do like hanging out with my buds." She slips her hand in mine. "And there's the Mental Club."

My hand feels like a limp noodle in hers. I try to act casual. I try not to look like I'm exploding inside.

Halle pulls me along, shuffling through as many leaves as she can, winding back and forth across the sidewalk as she kicks at them with the pointed toe of her Mary Jane shoes, as though she's practicing some ballet move. I try to keep up with her, but I only have one move and it's not that graceful.

She has on jeans that look expensive, the kind with jewels on the butt, and when she bends over to pick a yellow flower, I have to remind myself not to stare. "My favorite color," she says, twirling the flower in her hand as if she knows the color matches her voice.

We probably look strange strolling back and forth across the sidewalk, hand in hand. But this is one time I don't care what others think. I'd walk this way every day if it meant that Halle would let me hold her hand. What would she say if I told her who I was, if I reminded her that in kindergarten she got stung by a bee and her arm broke out in a rash and she had to go to the nurse's office? Or how in musical chairs it was down to her and me and I let her take the chair? Would she remember me? Would she remember how I recited the entire dialogue from a Pokémon movie she loved? Would it make a difference?

The words hang on my tongue, ready to slip out. But I derail them. I don't want anything to ruin this day. "Did you get in trouble with your dad?" I ask innocently.

Halle lets go of my hand and I immediately regret asking her that question. "You mean about our protesting? No big deal. He just said that next time we have to stay off the road."

"Oh."

"I mean, it's not like we did anything illegal. It's our right to protest. He understands that."

That's not what I heard yesterday at her window. She was crying and her dad was yelling at her. I can always tell when Mom is lying—her voice quivers just a bit. It's subtle, but I've noticed it since I was young. Maybe that's what I'm hearing in Halle's voice now. There's a tension to it, as though it's costing her something to tell this lie. Why isn't she being honest? And why does it bother me so much that she's not telling the truth when I've been dishonest from the start?

We walk past a nail salon and I see the red awning across the street. It's then that I realize where we're heading. I put my hand out.

"Wait. That's the Tin Cup Restaurant. My mom works there."

Halle stops. "Really? We'll have to go to Mel's Diner then. It's just around the corner."

She leads me around the block, taking the long route so we don't pass in front of Mom's restaurant.

"I have to warn you. Mel's is a dump," she says.

It takes a moment for my eyes to adjust to the darkened interior. We get our own menus from a front counter and sit in a booth away from the window.

The lunch specials are printed on a grease-lined piece of paper attached inside the menu. Mine has a dead fly stuck to it. Fried chicken and meatloaf are the specialties of the day.

A waitress sets down two plastic glasses filled with water, no ice. "An order of nachos with no meat," Halle says. "We're splitting them."

"Anything else?"

"Two Cokes," Halle says before I can open my mouth. I quickly add up the cost: five dollars and forty-nine cents for the nachos and one dollar nineteen cents for each of the Cokes. That's seven dollars and eighty-seven cents for the meal before tax with enough leftover for a small tip. Even though there might be some disagreement on whether or not this is a date, at least I can afford it.

There are eight other people in the restaurant. Halle picks up the plastic glass and swirls it around, focusing on the water. "The only thing edible here is the nachos. Definitely don't try the lefse. Everyone knows that Mabel Turner is the only person in Wellington who can make decent lefse and she only does it on special occasions down at St. John's Lutheran."

"What's lefse?"

Halle lets out a small laugh. "It's like a potato tortilla. Not that bad, really. Just don't let anyone talk you into trying lutefisk." She makes a sour face. "Jellied codfish. Need I say more?"

I put my hands up. "Please don't."

She takes a breath. "The Tin Cup has much better food."

I nod. "My mom brings home dinner three times a week. The shrimp scampi is the best I've ever had."

"Too bad your mom is working there. That makes it off limits for lunch. What do we have to avoid so we don't run into your dad?"

"He died when I was three."

"I'm sorry. You don't remember him then?"

I shrug. "I have some memories."

"Really? I can't recall anything that far back. I kind of remember living in California when I was little, but it's pretty vague."

I could refresh her memory.

She leans forward and says in a low voice, "So do you want the real lowdown on Wellington, Minnesota? Or do you prefer the Stepford version?"

I bend and our faces meet in the middle of the booth. Hers is inches away. This is the closest I've been to her since I kissed her back in kindergarten. I could reach over and kiss her now. I wonder what she'd do, if she'd kiss me back, or if she'd smack me in the mouth. Does she even think of me the way I think of her? Does she think of me at all?

"What's the truth about Wellington?"

"It has decent schools, but a lot of snow and you'll freeze your butt off here. The kids grow up and go off to good colleges and never come back. Period."

"So where do they go?"

"Bigger cities like Minneapolis or Chicago, or if they're smart they go south where it's warmer. We moved here when I was in kindergarten, but I'm going back to California some-day. Back to sunny, warm weather."

"Maybe you should check out colleges there." I picture us both at the same university. By then I'm sure Dink will have gotten himself into trouble again and be serving twenty years for another felony. At least I hope so.

The waitress sets our Cokes on the table. "Nachos are almost ready," she says, then leaves.

Halle picks up her straw and twirls it around her fingers. "I'm thinking of going to Portugal and doing something totally impulsive, like learning to be a cork stripper."

My eyes widen.

"It's not what you think, silly. They strip the bark from trees to make wine corks. Except that I have a problem with destroying trees, so that probably won't work. Did you know that *obrigado* is Portuguese for thank you?"

"No. I never studied Portuguese."

"I don't either; I just read that somewhere. I'll probably go to Princeton, actually. That's where F. Scott Fitzgerald gradu-ated. I'll let Daddy pay for it, then I'll write my own *Gatsby* about the lack of morality in companies like his."

"I thought *Gatsby* was a love story."

Halle's eyes smirk at me. "What chapter are you on?"

"Six. We're having a quiz tomorrow on chapters five and six."

"The chapter where Daisy and Tom attend Gatsby's party?"

I nod. "And where we learn about Gatsby's real identity, and how he transformed himself."

Halle takes a long sip of her Coke. "But he didn't. He conjured up this image at the age of seventeen, this persona that he thought he could pull off. Nothing lasts forever. In the end don't you think people will discover who he really is?"

Her words slice through me as though she's talking about me and not Gatsby. "Maybe it won't matter."

She shakes her head. "I don't want to throw you a spoiler, New Kid, but the truth always matters."

I know it's just a book, but I've come to identify with Jay Gatsby, with his love for a woman he knew years ago and his desire to win her over again. But now that I've been warned about Gatsby's future, it feels as though it's become wrapped up in my own, in my plot to reinvent myself into something I'm not. If a man as clever and handsome and single-minded as Gatsby couldn't succeed, then how am I going to?

In an instant, my dream date is shattered.

Pitching Hay Bales

"Use your arms** and legs, not your back."

I pick up another bale from the rack and haul it to the conveyer belt that carries it to the loft. I'm lucky to be able to move at all. I don't want to look like a wimp, but hauling fifty-pound bales of hay while sweat pours down my face for two hours straight is the hardest physical labor I've ever done. I have stalks in my hair, down my shirt and sock, and inside my work gloves, even in my pants. I itch all over. My arms no longer feel connected to my body.

I stop to rest at the end of the rack and take a swig of Gatorade. I'm not sure I'm going to make it.

"We're lucky Dad decided to make small bales," Brad says as he watches me. "They're usually seventy-five to one hundred pounds."

I drag myself over to him. "If you're saying that to make me feel better, then you suck."

Brad laughs. He has the same laugh as his dad, who picked us up after school in a dusty black pickup. They both sound like the color gray.

"I should mention that I've never worked on a farm before," I told his dad as his weathered hand grasped mine in a firm handshake.

"Lifting bales of hay isn't rocket science. But you're in for a good time," he joked with a hearty laugh. "Nothing builds muscle like farm work."

"If he survives," Brad said, and they both laughed.

When we pulled out of the school parking lot and drove past the football field, Brad turned his head to look at the empty field, a wistful expression on his face. I didn't ask him about it, but it's been on my mind since then.

"Is this what you do every day after school?" I ask.

"This time of year, yeah. It's not that bad. We all pitch in." Brad's older brother Karl is in the loft above us, moving bales off the conveyer belt. His dad mowed and raked the field a few days ago. He later drove across that same field with a tractor that pulled a baler, a machine that gathers the mowed hay and squirts it out in rectangular bundles. Brad's mom drove a truck pulling a flatbed rack from the field to the barn. It's stacked high with the hay bales. I can see his dad still out in the field past the grazing dairy cows, baling more hay, trying to make the most of the warm afternoon sun.

"What about sports?" I ask Brad.

"What about them?"

"I'd guess the football coach would love to have you on the roster."

" 'Course he would. I played when I was younger. Been too busy the last few years, though. I might play again when I feel like it."

I'm not sure why he doesn't feel like it now. He'd be a sure starter on the varsity team. But he turns away and I get the feeling I shouldn't press him.

We unload one rack as his mom pulls up with another one. I cringe at the piles of bales. Counting them would only depress me right now.

"There are snacks inside when you need a break," she says to me. "Don't overdo it this first day."

What I really want is to go home. Mom won't be picking me up for another hour and a half. And the bales aren't going anywhere, so Brad and I take a bathroom break. We walk through an old porch with cracked plaster and worn tile that looks a hundred years old, but it leads to a remodeled kitchen and living room that look eighty years newer.

"My grandpa grew up in this house," Brad says. "This farm has been in our family for over a hundred years."

We sit at the kitchen counter and eat homemade apple strudel. The soft apple and cinnamon mixture is still warm and I inhale three pieces.

Brad pours us glasses of milk. "My mom makes the best strudel."

I agree, even though it's the first time I've ever eaten it.

"So, you coming back after today?" he asks between bites.

"If my arms don't fall off."

He nods. "Good. I wasn't sure. I mean, you've got that California tan. I thought you might be trying out for the tennis team or something."

"I don't play tennis."

"Yeah, well, you seem the type."

"Do I seem the type to lift hay bales?"

"Hell, no."

"Then why'd you ask me to help?"

My question catches him off guard. He sputters out an answer. "I thought you might like some extra cash, and having help would make the job go faster."

"So you'd have more time for something else?"

"Like what?"

I shrugged. "I don't know. Football?"

Brad tips his Vikings cap. "How'd you know?"

"You don't seem the tennis type, either."

Brad smirks. "Okay, you're right. I really want to be on the team, but Dad needs me here. I thought that if we got ahead a bit, he might let me take some time off to play." He sighs. "Don't see that happening, though. What's your sport?"

"Well, I joined the Environmental Club."

He nods. "Yeah, you seem that type, too."

"I'm not, though. Not really," I confess. "I only joined to hang out with Halle Phillips."

"That's as good a reason as any, I guess. You know, before you go off on the environmental practices of our farm, I have to tell you that we do as much sustainable farming as we can. We use minimum pesticides and we don't fill our animals with a bunch of hormones. But we can't go organic and make a living here. Dad's barely scraping by as it is." He shakes his head. "You know how many farms are going under in this area? If we disappear, all that will be left are the big industrialized farms. So go tell your environmental club that." His voice is tight.

"I wasn't going to say anything about your farm," I respond. "Our club is protesting the taconite plant in town because of the number of people who've died from mesothelioma."

"I hate to tell you this, Baxter, but if the taconite plant closed down, there wouldn't *be* a town."

"That doesn't mean they shouldn't ensure the safety of the people who work there. All we're asking for is a study on the effects of the taconite dust on the workers."

Brad puts our plates in the dishwasher. "You sound awfully committed for someone who only joined to impress a girl."

He's right. I'm beginning to sound just like Halle and Eddie and the rest of them. Maybe I *should* take up tennis.

Brad pats me on the back as we return to work. "You're not that type, huh?"

The Plan and Halle's Ex

The next meeting of the Environmental Club is held in room 201 at 2:36 p.m., exactly one week after the protest. The five of us sit in a circle on top of the desks, passing around a bag of Fritos.

I hope we're going to discuss world hunger or global warming or something remote to northern Minnesota. I'm even thinking of bringing up the dragonflies if it will keep us away from the taconite plant.

But Halle is a broken record. She won't give up. "We need higher clean air standards in the plant. I mean, no one knows what level of exposure to taconite fibers is safe."

Eddie nods. "What we really need is a strategy. A way to make people sit up and notice the problem."

"It's more than that," Roxie adds. "We want action. My

aunt is a nurse and she said that she's seeing more cases of mesothelioma every year."

Gina hugs Eddie's arm. "I've got it. Let's call Oprah." Today she has a purple streak down the middle of her short, dark hair. It's a good match for her landing-strip voice.

"Get real," Eddie says, pushing his long hair behind his ears. "Oprah isn't interested in the Iron Range."

He has on the shirt with the big red-and-black turtle on the front. This time I read the back of it, which says, "Turtle Mountain Band of Chippewa Indians." All this time I'd thought Eddie was just into turtles.

"Gina has a point," Halle says. "Wouldn't it be great to have a celebrity get behind us? Someone big?"

"Oprah's big," Gina insists.

"We're not calling Oprah," Eddie says. "If we're going to get a celebrity, I'd rather go with someone hot. Someone with big breasts." He holds out his hands.

Gina slugs his arm. "Don't talk about women that way." But she looks down at her own shirt as she talks, as though checking to see how she measures up.

"What chance do we have to get someone like that anyway?" Roxie asks in a whispery voice. "Who's going to support the Madison High Mental Club going up against a big company like Wellington Mines?"

Gina opens her mouth, probably to say something about Oprah, but Eddie sticks a Frito in it. "She's right," Eddie said. "Nobody cares about what happens on the Iron Range. We're at the mercy of the foreign investors."

"The Department of Health," I blurt out. I want to

contribute, but my throat constricts at the thought of speaking up. I'm always worried I'll mess up.

"What about it?" Eddie asks.

I look to Halle. She nods her encouragement. "If a study was necessary, it would be done by the Department of Health."

Eddie shakes his head. "If the Department of Health cared about us, they'd have done a study years ago. You're on 'The Range' now. Blue-collar, beer-drinking, hell-raising miners and loggers who don't matter shit to the rest of the world except for how much iron we produce. You ever hear of us in California? Did you even know what the Iron Range was before you moved here? No, because we're in the middle of freakin' nowhere, USA."

"Lebanon, Kansas, is the geographic center of the United States," I correct him.

"What?" He stares at me as though I said I love Oprah.

"Don't harass the new kid," Halle warns. "We're not exactly garnering the support of our fellow students as it is."

She turns to me and whispers, "Lebanon, Kansas? Who knows that kind of stuff?"

That's nothing. I could tell her that I learned that piece of information on October 16 two years ago. I could tell her that I had toast with peanut butter and two glasses of milk for breakfast that morning and that a semi collided with a pickup truck and two cars thirty minutes later on the freeway east of our house. I could tell her the names of the three people who were killed.

Shakespeare said that "ignorance is the curse of God." He would have thought differently if he'd had my memory.

It's a problem of opening my mouth when I should just

leave it closed. When I first met Dr. Anderson, I tried to impress him by memorizing pages of the phone book in his office.

"How do you do that?" Dr. Anderson asked.

"I see them in my mind," I told him.

"I don't think you have a photographic memory, but you do have an amazing ability to remember."

"Why isn't it photographic?"

"Well, lots of people claim to have a photographic memory, but no one really does."

"I do," I insisted, as though I'd been presented with a challenge.

So Dr. Anderson did perform one test on me: the random dot stereogram test. He showed my right eye a pattern of ten thousand random dots, and the next day showed my left eye a different dot pattern. I mentally fused the two and saw an image of a three dimensional dinosaur, like one of those magic 3-D pictures that you have to cross your eyes to see. Afterward, Dr. Anderson said I had an authentic photographic memory.

I'd puffed up when Dr. Anderson had told me I was the only person who'd ever passed the test. He said it was a special gift, like having absolute musical pitch.

But someone with absolute pitch would know better than to belt out the lyrics of "Hey Jude" in the middle of the Environmental Club meeting. Why didn't I have that filter?

"Baxter is right," Roxie says. I'm surprised that her soft voice holds that kind of strength. "Look at us. We're a group of five. How much pressure can we put on Wellington Mines? But the Mesothelioma Research Association looks at these problems. They have some kind of environmental competition every year for school clubs like ours to encourage environmental awareness. But the deadline is just a few weeks away. If we could get them interested, maybe they'd put pressure on the Department of Health."

Halle frowns. "I don't know what kind of chance we'd have at a competition. But maybe if they think it's more than just a regional problem they'll do something. They're using leftover taconite tailings in road construction now. That affects everyone, not just the people of Wellington."

"How are we going to get anyone to come up here?" Gina asks. "I mean, without Hollywood or Oprah to help us?"

Eddie holds a finger in the air, silencing us. "That's it. We go Hollywood. We make a movie. We talk to the families, do a profile of the people who died and the cancer that caused their deaths. You know, our own Michael Moore film."

Gina grabs his finger. "Who's gonna talk to us?"

"We can talk to us." Halle's feet are shaking as they hang off the desk. "We start with ourselves. We've all lost someone to mesothelioma, except for Baxter." She looks at me and the energy pours off her like sweat. "We can use the video for the competition and you can film it, Baxter. You'll give the whole film a fresh perspective."

"Me? But I don't—"

"We can get the equipment from Kenny in the AV Department," Eddie says in a rushed voice. "Roxie, you look up the requirements for the competition. And you and Gina check out other families who've had relatives die of mesothelioma. Gina, you are my inspiration."

He kisses her on the neck and she giggles. "Not here, you savage."

He grumbles into her neck, "I love it when you talk dirty."

Roxie folds her arms. "What's this movie rated?"

"We'll take turns interviewing each other," Halle says. "We'll talk about our relatives who have died. Then we'll make a chart with facts and figures to back it up."

Halle and Eddie make plans to borrow the equipment and introduce me to the tech guy at school. Gina and Roxie will write out interview questions and do the research.

I walk outside with Halle at 4:07 after the meeting is over. The rest of our group is ahead of us.

"Don't worry about Eddie," she says. "He has a lot of rough edges."

"I don't think he likes me," I confess.

"Eddie doesn't like anyone at first. He says that he picks his friends carefully and his enemies even more carefully."

I can't help but wonder which category I'll end up in.

"No offense, Baxter, but you have a tendency to blurt out random things, so I figure you for more of a behind-the-scenes type of guy. I hope you don't mind not being in front of the camera."

"I don't care about that. But I've never made a movie before."

She takes my arm. Her touch feels natural, like it's meant to be there. I remember all the times we held hands in kindergarten, how natural it felt then, too. But it feels different now. More purposeful.

"Just think," she says. "You could become the next Scorsese and you'll owe it all to me. Then I can say I knew you before you were famous."

We step outside and a shiver works through me as the cold air fills my sweatshirt.

"How did it get so cold so fast?"

Halle puts her arms out wide. "Welcome to the land of extremes. Don't worry, you'll get used to it." Her voice takes the chill out of the air. It's captivating and breathless and it reminds me of the line from *Gatsby*, "that voice was a deathless song."

Being with Halle is a rush of emotion. Part of me wants to share everything with her, to tell her about kindergarten and Dink and my photographic memory and how she sounds like I imagine the garden of Eden sounded before God kicked out Adam and Eve. The other part wants to forget everything about Dink and my former life and be the guy she thinks I am, the guy she needs me to be.

We're almost at Eddie's van when a red and black motorcycle pulls up in front of us. Halle's grip on my arm tightens.

"Hi, Halle," a guy with square shoulders says from behind a black helmet. Then he takes it off and shakes out his blond tresses. It's Hunter, the ice hockey god. He sees Halle's hand, or what her hand is grabbing, and he revs the engine not once, but twice, and I have a feeling I'm making another enemy.

"Hey, Hunter. Why aren't you hitting a hockey puck?" Halle sounds friendly enough, but I'm relieved when I don't hear the bubbly in her voice.

"We got out early today. You need a ride?"

"No thanks."

"You still trying to save the world?"

"Just the Iron Range. I'm putting off Asia and Africa till senior year."

He laughs. "You always crack me up." Then he nods at me. "You new?"

Halle tugs on my arm. "This is Baxter. He moved here from California and no, he's not a hockey puck addict like you. At least, I don't think so. Are you, Baxter?"

I flex my arm, feeling the strain on my new muscles from a week of baling hay. It hurts like the devil. I'd like to say that I play hockey, but I'm enough of a fake as it is. "I don't know how to skate."

Hunter smirks at this. "Everyone knows how to skate."

I shrug like it's no big deal but what I'd really like to do is wipe that smirk off his face.

Hunter winks at Halle. "So, we have an exhibition game in a couple of weeks. You gonna support the home team?"

Halle tips her head. "Oh, I'm sure you have all the support you need. You know? Like Jenna?"

Hunter flinches at Jenna's name. "Jenna's okay, but she's kind of an airhead. I'd really like it if you came. For old time's sake?"

Halle twists her hand around mine. "We'll try to make it if we're not tied to a tree somewhere."

"Yeah. Well, see you at lunch tomorrow, Halle. And if you need a ride to school, gimme a call." Then he winks at me.

"Jerk," Halle says when he leaves. She squeezes my hand before she lets go. "I didn't do that to make him jealous or anything. I just don't want him to think he's got a second chance with me. He didn't know that Jenna's so possessive. Poor Hunter. He's going to have a hard time getting rid of her."

The feel of Halle's hand in mine was a perfect fit, and my

hand tingled when she let go, as though some of her magic has rubbed off on me.

Brad was right. I don't have a lot of time. Hunter's already making a move. Maybe it's just my anger at him acting so confident and condescending, but I decide to make a bold move back. I take her hand in mine again. "I'm not sure he got the message."

Halle's eyebrows shoot up, two thin lines of surprise. She smiles and squeezes my hand. "Then I guess we'll have to convince him."

A Message

On the ride home Halle babbles more about the movie. I use the word "babble" because I can't really pay attention to anything she's saying while we're holding hands. I look away nervously, hoping mine isn't getting too sweaty. This is way different from kindergarten. For one thing, there wasn't a lump in my throat at the thought of being this close to Halle when I was five. Not only are our hands laced together, but our legs are touching. When the van takes a rough corner, she leans into me; her hair brushes my cheek. I'm so glad Eddie takes the corners fast.

"Grandpa used to tell me that one person can make all the difference in the world. I'm glad we're doing this. It sounds weird, but I feel like he's helping us, you know?"

"You must have been close," I manage to reply. Flashes of my grandpa appear in my mind; a thin, balding man with tight lips and a constant irritation in his eyes that made him blink constantly. He never had much to say to me, and his spare conversation with Mom seemed to always lead to an argument with her storming out of the room.

Halle's eyes fill with wetness when she talks about her grandfather, and the daffodils in her voice stand up taller. I envy her.

Eddie drops me off first. "See you tomorrow," I say as I get out, reluctantly letting go of Halle's hand. She waves and I back away, almost stepping on the rake Mom left out front in her enthusiasm to do fall raking. I stop near the tree, pick at some brown leaves, and peek as they drive down the street.

When I get inside, I check the clock above the sink. It's two minutes slow. I stand on a kitchen chair and reach up to change the clock to match my watch. I'm on the chair when it occurs to me: obsessing over time like this is only going to make me look strange, or stranger than I already am. I have a girlfriend now. Okay, we only held hands, but there's potential and I don't want to do anything to blow it. I turn the clock back the way it was before and get off the chair.

I've never felt this way: giddy and lightheaded and . . . happy. I've never been so happy before. Dink is thousands of miles away; I'm sure of it, and tomorrow I'll see Halle again.

I think about calling to see if Halle got home all right. It's been seven minutes since they dropped me off. Kind of a lame excuse for wanting to talk to her. And I'm not really good at small talk. Which makes me wonder why Halle would be interested in me in the first place. She's intense, focused, and outspoken. Not to mention rich and beautiful.

I'm not bad-looking and I'm starting to bulk up from lifting hay bales, but my tan is fading and I'm not athletic. As far as Halle knows, I struggle in class and need a tutor. We're not close to rich, even if I count the sixty-five thousand, three-hundred fifty-eight dollars and ninety-seven cents that I stole from Dink.

The giddiness fades quickly.

I remember how Gatsby tried so hard to impress Daisy, of how she cooed and cried at his collection of shirts, and I wonder what I can do to impress Halle that way. I don't have a big mansion, or even a motorcycle like Hunter. All I have is the money in my closet and the ten dollars an hour I'm earning at Brad's. Maybe I should buy Halle a gift. Something that would make her happy. Something that would impress her.

That's when I notice the light flashing on the phone. I tap the message button, wishing that Halle had somehow already called, even though I know that's not possible. Or maybe it's Brad telling me I don't have to work this weekend after all. My arms tighten just at the thought of lifting another bale of hay.

"Hi there." The muddy voice sounds fake friendly. I gasp at the sound, as if his voice has reached right into our kitchen and grabbed my throat. He knows our phone number! How did he get our phone number?

"I know you probably don't want to talk to me, but three years have given me time to think, and I just want to say hi from California. I'm sorry, Mary. I think we have some things that we need to talk about if you're willing. Oh, and I'd like to talk to you too, Baxter. Bye now."

I reach over as though the machine is possessed and press

the delete button. It's a gut reaction, anything to get rid of that sound. If he has our phone number, what else does he have? Does he know where we live? Should we move again?

I put my head in my hands, trying to think. I could just send him the money. He'd probably leave us alone if I did that. Crap! We can't move now that I've found Halle again. I'm just starting to make a new life for myself and Dink has to go and mess it up.

I stare at the machine, wishing I could make it all go away. I was so happy just a few minutes ago. I'm not telling Mom, not until I've had a chance to think it through.

I check the money again. It's still there. Then I check all the locks on the doors and sit down to do my math homework at the kitchen table, but Dink's voice keeps breaking in. Mom comes home at 5:17 according to my watch; 5:15 according to the clock on the wall. She's carrying two white plastic containers.

I look up from the linear equation worksheet. I've never been so grateful to see her. I try to keep my voice even. "Chicken and rice night."

Mom has a sly smile on her face. "I knew you'd remember that, so I brought home something else." She places the containers on the table and I open one. A pork tenderloin sandwich and the Tin Cup's famous seasoned fries cut into oval shapes. I like chicken and rice better, but I have to give her points for originality.

"Surprise!" she shouts. Only my mom could get so excited about surprising me with food.

"Is anything wrong?" she asks, because even when I think I'm doing a great job of hiding my emotions, Mom can always tell.

"No. Just tired."

"Maybe you're working too hard, taking on too much."

"No. Our meeting got over early today."

"So how did it go?" she asks.

"Okay." I stuff fries into my mouth.

"What do you do there? I've never even heard of an environmental club."

"We're making a movie. I'm the cameraman."

"A movie? About what?"

"Mesothelioma. It's a cancer caused by the taconite dust in the mines."

"What happened to the dragonflies?"

I pause. "They're still there."

I stuff more food in my mouth, but Mom isn't eating. She's watching me.

"What?" I ask through a mouthful.

"Nothing. I'm glad you took my advice and got involved."

"It's just a club." I don't want her to get too excited. We might have to move soon. The thought makes my stomach grow tight, knowing it could all disappear. The school, the friends, the club. I swallow a lump of bread. Even Halle. Dink is a looming threat that overshadows everything.

"I know. But we need people in our lives. You do. And so do I."

I stop eating. The sandwich is poised in front of my mouth. "What people do you need?"

She fingers her sandwich, pulling out pieces of lettuce. "Oh,

I don't know. All sorts of people. I'm making friends at work. And I'm thinking of taking an art class at the community college."

Oh. I relax and take a bite. "That's good."

Mom puts down her sandwich and wipes the crumbs from her hands. She clears her throat. "Okay, don't get upset. I have a date next week."

I almost choke on my sandwich. "A date?"

"Well, it's not a date, really. My boss asked me to go to a new club opening on the other side of town."

"Oh. What's your boss like?" I can already feel the tension building, the familiar tightness in the pit of my stomach. I think of Dink, of how he seemed nice when I first met him and what a jerk he turned out to be. He's the reason we moved to Minnesota. You'd think Mom would learn. But here she is, considering dating again.

"He's responsible and has a good sense of humor, but he doesn't tell stupid jokes all the time. And he's not uptight like . . ." she stops and shakes her head. Maybe it's that easy for her to get rid of Dink, just shake her head and he disappears forever. It's not that easy for me.

I almost tell her then. I want to blurt out the whole story, to tell her about the money, to warn her against ever dating another guy, because her last boyfriend ruined our lives.

"So, what do you think?" she asks me.

"What do I think? This is what I think." I throw down my sandwich, grab my books, and stomp to my room.

Tackling Football Players

"**We don't hear** Gatsby's voice until chapter three. We don't learn about his childhood until chapter six. Then in chapter seven we find out about his criminal dealings. Why do you think the author waited that long to reveal his character?"

Mr. Shaw walks back and forth in front of the classroom. His blue T-shirt flashes between the desks like a piece of California sky. I've been thinking about California since last night, wondering if Dink is still there or driving his beat-up Camaro to Minnesota. What would Dr. Anderson say about the sixty-five thousand, three-hundred fifty-eight dollars and ninety-seven cents I took? Would he say I'm a criminal like Dink who deserves to be locked up, too?

I was awake most of the night. Every little noise pricked my skin: the click of the lock when Mom turned the bolt on the front door, the uneven hum of the refrigerator, the wind hissing through a window, the creak of my bedsprings. I imagined Dink in my closet, the money in his hand, ready to pounce. We left California to get away from Dink, but he's here, behind every corner and closed door.

"Baxter, do you agree with John?"

I look up blankly. "I have no idea what John said."

Sudden laughter explodes behind me. Mr. Shaw nods as though he knows I haven't been paying attention. I hate when teachers do that. "John said that one of the reasons Fitzgerald waited that long to reveal Gatsby's character was to keep up the suspense. Would you agree?"

I'm tired. Not in the mood for a discussion. Especially not in the mood to keep up this charade.

"Yes. I agree." My voice is monotone.

But Mr. Shaw won't let me off easy. "Why?"

I sigh. "Gatsby is a celebrity, a rich man who throws lavish parties, but no one knows anything about him. So all these rumors and gossip fill the first part of the book, and that's part of the mystery of Gatsby. He becomes a legend before we even meet him."

Brad flashes me a thumbs-up sign. Mr. Shaw nods as he passes by my desk. His blue jeans rub up against my backpack. "So this legend of a man formulated his own blind conception of Daisy, who represents the dream that he created 'Jay Gatsby' to achieve. Why can't he see her for who she is?"

The girl in front of me, Louise, raises her hand. "Because he still thinks of her as the girl he fell in love with all those years ago?"

"Exactly. And because he has this false concept of her,

he doesn't accept that she will never desert her own class and background to be with him."

"That's stupid on her part," I blurt out.

Mr. Shaw stops behind me. "What?"

I know I should keep quiet, but I can't help myself. "She would have been better off with Gatsby instead of her lying, cheating husband."

Mr. Shaw sticks his hands in his pockets. "We'd like to believe that, but I'm wondering if their affair wasn't doomed from the start. Even with Gatsby's money, he didn't have the social class that her husband had. And that was important to Daisy."

"She loved Gatsby," I insist.

Louise looks at me as she speaks. "But in chapter seven she can't decide between the two. If she really loved him, wouldn't she have told her husband to take a flying leap off the end of the dock?"

"Yeah," Brad adds. "And didn't she promise to wait for Gatsby when he proposed? Then she goes and marries this other dude the minute he's gone. Seems like she was a big flirt."

"She does appear to be fickle, doesn't she?" Mr. Shaw agrees. He leans against his desk and runs his hand through his beard, a slight smile on his face.

I shouldn't get so worked up about this, but I feel as though it's me being attacked and not Gatsby. My breath comes in short spurts, building up inside.

I grab my book and stand. "No! She was just confused. She tells Gatsby she loves him. On page 116, 'As he left the room again she got up and went over to Gatsby and pulled his face down, kissing him on the mouth. "You know I love you," she murmured.'"

"Oh my God. You memorized that? That's so weird," Louise says, and her eyes mock me.

"Why is it weird? Because you can't?"

"What do you mean? Who'd *want* to memorize it?"

Jeb Danner, a JV football player, laughs. "What did you do? Memorize the whole book?"

The entire class bursts into laughter. I feel every eye turn toward me and I shrink back down into my chair.

"No," I say, but who can hear me through the laughter?

"That's enough!" Mr. Shaw quiets the class.

The bell rings. "Great discussion," he says. "Read the last two chapters for Thursday and be prepared for a pop quiz."

"We don't have to memorize it, do we?" Louise asks, and the class laughs again.

Brad nudges my shoulder. "Don't be mad, dude. They're just teasing. I mean, it's cool that you're into the book."

I grab my backpack and hurry from the room. My chest feels tight as I run down the hallway.

I pull out *Gatsby* and start reading even as students spill into the hallway and brush against me. I'd put it down last night because I was tired. Or maybe I hadn't wanted to read the ending. I wanted to believe that Jay Gatsby and Daisy end up together, that Halle and I will end up together even though Hunter is a sports jock who drives a motorcycle and has more money than me and is an upperclassman and is clearly into Halle by the way he spoke to her. I want to believe that I can get Dink out of our lives and out of my head, that I can live a normal life like everyone else, that I can stop the memories from replaying like a bad sitcom for the rest of my life.

Someone bumps into me and knocks the book out of my hands. It hits the ground and slides across the floor, and I lose sight of it among the trampling feet. I push my way through the crowd to retrieve it and smack into four guys walking by.

"Watch it!" they yell and shove me back against the lockers. My elbow hits metal, sending a searing pain up my arm. That's when I lose it. No words come out. Just a primal scream from somewhere deep inside. A scream against them and Dink and everyone who has ever done something to me that made me mad, and I can remember every single episode, every injustice, every hurtful comment. Just as they start to replay in my head, I explode. I have to get them out.

I run full force at the four guys in the midst of a wall of students. I jump and land against them. The impact knocks two of them over with me falling on top.

Other students trip over us and fall on the human pile. The heel of a shoe hits my ear, bringing a sharp pain. A knee crushes into my back and I gasp. Papers fly in the air.

I try to get up. My arms are lost among books and backpacks and limbs. Students are screaming. A girl shrieks and hits me in the stomach when my hand accidentally grasps her leg for support.

"What's going on?" A voice that sounds like a tank scatters the crowd. The knee is hoisted from my back. A hand grabs my shirt and pulls me up. I turn and see one of the deans.

"He started it," a guy yells and points at me. "He body-slammed us."

I'm waiting for the dean to let go of my shirt, but his hand stays put and he guides me into his office along with the kid who ratted me out.

I'm deposited into a chair. My ears are hot. The adrenalin flows through my body like water. I want to run, to go far away from this place, where Dink can never get into my head, where the memories will just stop for a while. But they don't.

Mom picked me up early from the Institute on a Wednesday afternoon.

"What are you doing here today?" Usually she picked me up early every other Thursday so I could meet with Mrs. Rupe, my therapist.

"I thought we'd go out for an early dinner. How about Rogio's? Your favorite."

"Yeah. Sure." Already my heart was racing. I mean, your mom doesn't take you out to your favorite restaurant unless she has some news. Something great or terrible to tell you. I racked my brain to think of any good news she might possibly have.

"Did you get a raise?"

"No. Can't I take my favorite boy to dinner?"

"Is Grandpa okay?"

"He's fine, Baxter. Don't be such a worrywart." But her voice quaked. I had reason to worry.

It wasn't until I'd inhaled a dozen breadsticks and their special tortellini alla primavera and she was paying the check that she broke it to me. Dink was getting released from prison early. It'd only been three years. But it's white collar crime and he had been a model inmate.

Mom should have waited until we got home. I screamed and stood up so fast that I knocked over the table. Breadsticks flew across the floor and sauce splattered Mom's purse.

"We have to get out of here. We have to move!" My hands were flying everywhere. The other patrons were cringing and the waiters were trying to back me into a corner, but I wouldn't go. Nothing could calm me down. Mom finally got her arms around me and squeezed me until I relaxed.

"We'll move, Baxter. We'll move far away from here if that's what you want," she said into my shirt.

"Mr. Green!" The man shouts my name and I'm back in the dean's office. How long has he been talking? How long have I zoned out this time?

"I just wanted to get my book," I say.

"Then why'd you tackle *me*?" the older kid asks. He has on an orange-and-black letter jacket. "I didn't have your book."

"You pushed me."

"No, I didn't."

"Yes, you did."

"Enough!" The dean has a thick neck. His face is red from yelling and his necktie is so tight it looks as though it's cutting off the air supply to his brain. "The disciplinary action for fighting in school is suspension."

"But I wasn't fighting," the other guy objects. "I was on my way to football practice when he jumped us for no reason. Ask Zach Mennen. He saw it. Honest, Mr. Jackson. Coach Smalley is going to be mad if I'm late."

"I was attempting to retrieve my book," I say through gritted teeth.

Mr. Jackson leans back against his desk. His face relaxes; his composure returns. "Scott, you go ahead to practice. I'll deal with you later."

Scott jumps up and sprints past me; a blur of orange and black. Right before he goes out the door, he turns and grins. I'm left with Tank Voice staring down at me.

The room is silent. I study the walls decorated with orange and black tigers, ones with sharp fangs dripping blood. Is it meant to scare students? Outside his office is the sound of laughter and voices that meld together; one voice sounds like a rectangle, another sounds like a poached egg.

"I didn't do anything wrong," I say. "Why did he get to go and I'm stuck here with you?"

Mr. Jackson puts up his hand. "As your dean, Mr. Green, I see that I should have met with you before. You obviously don't understand the rules and regulations of our school."

He stands. He's tall and solid, the type of guy who looks like he played football when he was younger. I decide he's against me from the start.

"I understand the rules and regulations. Does your football star understand them?"

"You're out of line."

"No, I'm pissed."

"You can be pissed in detention."

Mr. Jackson picks up a thick pamphlet from his desk. "I want this year to be a good one for you, but you're starting off on the wrong foot. Since you're new, I won't suspend you. *This* time. However, make no mistake, if it happens again, you'll receive the maximum penalty."

Tank Voice shakes his head and hands me the pamphlet. "I'm giving you a week's detention, starting today. You'll use that time to learn every single rule and regulation of Madison

High School. All one hundred and twenty-five pages. And next week, you will report back to me to answer questions about those rules and regulations."

Mr. Jackson stares down at me as though he's given me the worst punishment anyone could imagine.

I put my head down and hide a smirk.

Tank Voice claps his hands together. "That will be all, Mr. Green."

When It's Okay to Cheat

It's three o'clock and I'm supposed to be heading to meet Bob Schraan, the media guy, to show me how to use the camera. Instead I'm going to detention. It's not fair.

On my way to the room, I spot my book. It's crammed next to a locker, spread facedown. I pick it up and brush it off. The cover looks as though it's been smashed in a car door, but at least no pages are missing.

Room 121 is on the first floor, near the senior lockers. Luckily, no seniors are around. Upperclassmen are such jerks.

"Hey," Eddie calls out. He's standing at an open locker two doors down from the detention room. "You on your way to meet Bob? I'll show you where he hangs out."

"Um, sorry. I can't meet him today. Something came up." I glance at the door to the detention room.

Eddie's eyes shift from me to the door. "Detention? You? What'd you do, forget your homework too many times?"

"I knocked some guys down."

Eddie's eyes widen. "That was you? I heard someone made a flying leap into the defensive end of the football squad. You got a lot of nerve, kid."

Detention doesn't seem so bad now. At least Eddie is impressed.

" 'Course, you're gonna need a bodyguard from now on to make it through the halls without getting killed. The football team is tight with one another."

"Oh." The first-floor bathroom episode flashes through my mind. Those guys were probably friends of the ones I tackled. "Do you know any? Bodyguards, I mean."

Eddie laughs. "None that you'd want to be associated with. My advice is to maintain a low profile. Hey, just keep coming to the Environmental Club. No one even knows we exist." He nods toward the door. "How long you in for?"

"A week."

He shakes his head. "That's not going to work. The deadline for the competition is in three weeks and we want to submit the video. You haven't learned the equipment yet."

"A camcorder? How hard can it be?"

"Harder than you think, moron. It's a digital video recorder. We planned on you helping with the editing, too."

"I'll talk to Halle tomorrow and explain."

"It's not just Halle. It's all of us. We may be a joke at school, but we take our club seriously. We want a decent video, not some lame junior-high version. You haven't seen how people die of lung problems and cancer, and . . ." He stops and points a finger at me. "If you're just in this because you're hot for Halle Phillips, then stick to tackling football players and forget the Environmental Club."

Eddie's mood changes faster than the Minnesota weather.

My face heats up at the mention of Halle. "I want to be in the club," I assure him.

Eddie shifts his backpack onto his shoulder. "If you say so." But his voice is filled with doubt. "Tell you what. I'll get you the user manual to read in detention. It's not the same, but it will help. Then maybe you can meet with Bob before school."

"Thanks." Eddie doesn't like me. Maybe because he thinks I'm a fake. And he's right. I'm only in the club because of Halle. It's not that I don't care about the environment, but if Halle were into basketball or volleyball I'd pretend to be the biggest fan in the world just to impress her.

I watch him walk away. What kind of stake does Eddie have in the Environmental Club? Who did he lose? He never talks about it.

Eight other students sit in the detention room, each spaced out in a different row. They're all guys except one girl I recognize from Science. She usually sleeps in class, and her head dips back as she struggles to stay awake now. Her science book perches half-open on her desk.

The teacher is a heavy, gray-haired woman I don't know. She's knitting a pink-and-blue blanket while her eyes dart back and forth around the classroom. She flashes a menacing look at me and tells me to sit three seats behind the guy in the front row.

"Remember, this is detention," she says in a low voice. "Don't cause any ruckus. You make me miss a stitch and you'll have hell to pay. Understand?"

"Yes, ma'am."

"And I'd recommend you take better care of your books," she adds, nodding at the battered copy of *Gatsby* in my hand.

It's 2:57. I'll call Mom for a ride and she'll have to sign my detention form. After I got mad and left the dinner table last night, well, she's not in the best mood. We barely spoke this morning.

And then there's Dink. I still haven't told Mom he called. But right now I'm keeping Dink on the back burner of my thoughts. I have to convince Halle that I'm serious about helping her with the video. I have to make her understand that I'm not a slacker and that I'm worthy of her time and attention. And I have to finish reading *Gatsby* for the exam tomorrow.

I stare down at the worn copy. Suddenly, I can't bring myself to open the book. It might turn out badly for Jay Gatsby, and I don't need that kind of negative energy right now.

Instead I look out the window. The wind is picking up. In the distance the girls' soccer team kicks balls around the field, their ponytails flapping against their heads.

The only sounds in the detention room are the clicking of knitting needles, random coughs, pencils scribbling across paper, and pages turning. After a sleepless night, my eyelids feel weighted down. I struggle to stay awake. When I let my guard down, the memories take over.

Once a month on Friday afternoon, our third-grade teacher let us have "game day." She had a long shelf filled with games; Monopoly, Scrabble, Clue, checkers, Battleship. She even had a deluxe edition of Trivial Pursuit. There was a boy in my class, Jack Pelazzo, who had crooked teeth and a bad temper. I beat him at Trivial Pursuit three months before and he called me a cheater and hadn't played me again since, but he'd done everything he could to make my life miserable. He poked me in the back when we were standing in line for lunch. He stole my pencils when I wasn't looking. He threw the basketball and hit me in the head during Phys Ed, then pretended it was an accident.

On Friday when we were sorting through games, he picked up the deluxe edition of Trivial Pursuit and grabbed my arm. "Hey, cheater, I'll give you a rematch and a chance to win fair and square."

"I already won fair and square."

"You afraid to play me?"

I wasn't about to back down, so we played again, and this time he won, but I was positive he cheated. I wondered if he stacked the cards for himself. He made such a big deal about it afterward and acted like a snob. It really made me mad. So I stayed inside the next day during recess to work on my math problems, but instead I read all the Trivial Pursuit cards.

Jack never beat me again. At first it made me happy, but eventually I felt guilty. Jack chased me around the school yard calling me a cheater. It stung more than usual because this time I was one, sort of. I read all the answers. Having a memory that doesn't forget felt like cheating.

"I have something for Baxter." Eddie's voice thrusts through the memory. He stands just outside the classroom door. The woman with the knitting needles looks at me, sighs, and nods her head toward the door.

I stand up, still feeling out of breath from my chase around the school yard, as though it had just happened. Eddie hands me the directions to the school video camera, a pamphlet as thick as the school rules.

"Happy reading," he says in a sarcastic voice. "Halle wants to start filming on Wednesday."

"I'll be ready," I say. And I will. Memorizing the directions isn't the same as reading the answers to a game. It's not cheating if you're doing it to impress the girl of your dreams, is it?

Half a Lie

Mom dumps her purse on the table. She noisily opens the cupboard and takes out a pan, then bangs it down on the stove. She hasn't said a single word on the way home. Her back is rigid and straight.

"This isn't like before," I say.

"No, it's not. You used to get detention for talking back to your teacher. Now you're getting detention for fighting."

"See? This is an improvement."

She chops an onion and sprinkles pieces in the pan. They sizzle in the oil. Mom's cooking has improved since she started working at the restaurant; she's making chicken stir-fry tonight. My stomach growls in anticipation.

"School is going well," I insist. "It was just a misunderstanding."

"I hope you're right about that," she says in a tight voice.

"Because I really like it here and I don't want to move again. Maybe you should quit the club and job so you can focus on school."

"It's not a problem, Mom. I can handle it."

She turns back to the stove. Her shoulders loosen and she shifts her weight as she adds chopped peppers to the pan.

I know I should go do my homework. Leave her alone and let her calm down. But she can't take away the things that make me happy. They're all I have. "It won't happen again," I say in my most convincing voice. She's probably still mad at my reaction to her upcoming date. She's using it against me just because I got in a little trouble.

Mom sighs and turns around. "I'm just worried about you, Baxter. I want you to succeed at school. I don't want anything or anyone . . ." Her voice trails off.

"Anyone?" Does she know about Halle?

She wipes her hands on a towel. "I don't want you to freak out, but I think you should know. I spoke to Dink today."

My hands immediately begin to shake. "*Why?*" I scream. "*How?*"

She reaches over to take my hand, but I pull it away. "He called. Baxter, don't worry. I didn't tell him where we are. He has no idea."

"Really? Then how did he get our phone number?"

"I don't know, but—"

"I can't believe you actually talked to him!" I pace back and forth between the refrigerator and table. My heart feels like a ticking time bomb ready to explode. My mind is racing, fighting as images of Dink press in.

"We have to move again. Some place farther away," I say, although I can't imagine where that would be. Maybe the East Coast? I open the cupboards and start pulling out dishes.

Mom turns off the stove. "Stop it! We don't have to move. It isn't like that. He was calling from California. He's on probation so he can't leave the state. He can't even leave the city. And there's no reason for him to come here, anyway."

I glare at her. "You know how I feel about him."

Mom starts crying. I hate it when she cries; it always makes me feel guilty. "You're not the only one he hurt, Baxter."

I grit my teeth. "Then why would you want to talk to him?"

Mom puts her hands together like she's praying. "Before, I was so angry that all I wanted to do was forget Dink existed. But I've had more time to think. And when he called I realized that I needed to talk to him in order to put the past behind me once and for all."

She takes a yellow cup out of my hand and sniffs. "I'm not going to say I don't have feelings for him. I probably always will. But I'm not stupid. No matter what he says, I'll never, ever get back together with him. And he understands that. So we don't have to move. Okay?"

I let out a long breath. "I don't think he wants to get back together with you, Mom. He wants to get at me."

She shakes her head. "No. He kept talking about how bad he feels for what he did to you. How he wishes he could just talk to you and explain. That doesn't sound like someone who wants revenge."

It sounds exactly like Dink. Mom has no idea how

manipulative he can be. She needs to know. I have to tell her. "But he does want revenge."

"For what? Talking to the police and testifying against him? You were a child. You were just twelve years old. You didn't understand what was going on."

"Not for that. He wants revenge because he . . . he *thinks* I stole his money."

"What money?" Mom's voice jumps two octaves.

"Money he had hidden in his desk. He thinks I stole sixty-five thousand, three hundred fifty-eight dollars and ninety-seven cents."

I reach out to catch the cup as it falls from her hand, but I miss. It hits the floor, shattering into hundreds of tiny yellow pieces that fly across the green tile, and I can't help but think that they look like pieces of shredded daffodils.

How Confrontation Leads to Lying

If I tell her I have the money she'll think I'm the worst son ever. I take out a broom and start sweeping up pieces of glass. Mom grabs the handle.

"What do you mean he thinks you stole money from him? Why would he think that?"

"Because he's Dink. Because he's a jerk."

"No," she shakes her head. "He never said anything to me about it. He didn't have that kind of money."

"He did."

"How do you know how much money it was?" Her voice is accusatory.

I hate lying. But I've kept this secret so long that I can't tell Mom the whole truth now. "I saw it. In an envelope in his desk."

"Why didn't you tell me? What did you do with it?"

My heart is racing. The words come out in a rush. "I didn't want to get in trouble. I wasn't supposed to be looking in his desk, so I left it there."

"So where did it go?"

"How would *I* know?"

"Oh my God." Mom looks like she's just been slapped in the face. She obviously didn't know that Dink was squirreling away money. Mom wrings her hands and takes my place pacing the kitchen. If she's this upset, how would she react if she knew the money is in my closet in the guitar case right now?

"Maybe the police found it. Maybe he turned it over to them," she says more to herself than to me. But her eyes are full of doubt.

"The man never had money to help pay rent," she mumbles in an angry voice. "How did I let myself get into that mess? Why did I put up with him?"

My question exactly.

She bites down on her lip. "Why does Dink think *you* took it?"

More lies. It's like a house on stilts, but the stilts are made of cheap wood that will eventually split apart and the whole house will come tumbling down. I'm still not good at lying, and as I spit out the words now I can feel a drop of sweat slide down the side of my face. "Because I gave the police the papers with the numbers I wrote. I took it out of that same envelope."

She closes her eyes and rubs the bridge of her nose. "Are you sure Dink thinks you took his money? Maybe you misunderstood."

She looks tired. If she has a migraine now, it's going to get a whole lot worse.

"He talked to me at the trial, Mom. At the end. He said, 'I know you took something from me. You have my money, don't you?' Remember that?"

She shakes her head. "No."

Of course she doesn't remember. She had a thousand other thoughts and feelings going through her at that time. She thought Dink was ranting because he'd just been found guilty. She never imagined he was talking about something else.

"You're sure he said that," she says again, but it's not really a question. She knows I remember Dink's exact words. Doesn't she know that I'd forget them if I could?

She nods, her eyes still closed. Then she straightens up and sticks out her chin. "Don't worry. I'll take care of this."

But her voice quivers when she says that. I have reason to worry.

How Confrontation Leads to Kissing

We decide to get an unlisted phone number. It's not a real solution, but it makes us both feel better. Mom is positive that Dink doesn't know where we live, that even if he looks up our area code it will only give a general vicinity, and he's prohibited from leaving the county or the state. None of that makes me feel better.

I retreat to my bedroom. I hate how Dink is still affecting our lives after we moved two thousand miles away. I hate that I can't escape the memories of him and that I have to worry about him every day. I shouldn't have stolen the money. But it's too late to do anything with it now. And even if it's not too late, I don't want to give it to Dink.

I'm not going to let him ruin my life. I'm not going to spend it looking over my shoulder. I repeat this to myself until

I believe it. Then I do my math homework, all of it, even showing my work on the problems like Mr. Feege wanted.

After that, I read two chapters of Science and analyze the relationship between the structural characteristics of atoms and how atoms bond to form molecules. The whole time I'm working on my other homework, the copy of *Gatsby* stares up at me, patiently waiting its turn. I have to read the ending tonight so I can take the test tomorrow. I decide that no matter what happens in the book, I'll take it like a man. After all, Jay Gatsby is a fictional character and I'm real. That should be enough to put aside all the similarities I find between myself and the lonely rich man who changed his name in order to transform his dreams into reality.

I'm beginning to know what it's like to have a secret identity. Mine's not as mysterious as Gatsby's, but it's just as fake and just as hard to keep up. The memories are intruding more often. The stress continues to build. And today I lost it. I let my emotions loose like a rolling barrel onto the defensive end of the football team. It wasn't a pretty sight. My elbow smarts from the memory.

I have to keep it together. I have to be whatever Halle Phillips wants in a boyfriend, and I'm pretty sure that she wants a boyfriend who does his homework, who isn't a slacker, and who doesn't get in fights at school.

That's why I'm going in to school early on Monday to learn about editing and filming. And it's why I have to finish reading *Gatsby*. I'll do anything to please Halle.

So I finally pick up the book, kick off my shoes, and settle back against the grainy headboard of my bed to finish the last thirty-three pages.

Forty-five minutes later I throw the book against the wall.

"Fitzgerald is a crappy, immature coward!" I flop back on my pillow. It isn't fair. Books are supposed to see the possibilities that life doesn't offer, to give us happy, fairy-tale endings.

But that didn't work out for Gatsby and Daisy. I think of Dink, who used us and threw us away because of his greed. I think of all the people who rejected me because I wasn't like them. Are people today different than the ones in this book? Has society changed at all since 1920?

Halle is different. She has to be. But I wonder if I mean anything at all to her, or if she's just flirting with me to get even with Hunter. I have to find out. I want to know if she'll reject me in the end, even if I spend sixty-five thousand dollars trying to impress her.

At 10:08 I put on my shoes and a hooded sweatshirt and sneak out the back door into the cold darkness. It's creepy dark out, and I'm afraid I'll see Dink around every corner, but I keep walking purposefully toward Halle's house without any thought of what I'll say when I get there, except to confront her with the book in my hand, the one that foretells her betrayal.

It's 10:43 when I turn down Willow Way, the winding street with manicured lawns that remind me of the ones in *Gatsby*. The thought spurs me onward, until I'm standing in front of the turreted mansion, pounding on her door. When Halle opens it, the sight of her takes my breath away. Her hair is pulled into two short pigtails and she has on an oversized T-shirt that ends at her thighs.

"Baxter, what are you doing here?" she asks.

She's beautiful, but it's her irresistible voice that draws me in like a Pied Piper. The sound flutters in the air as though a field of daffodils is waving in the wind, thousands of them dancing in my head. I've never had alcohol before, but this is how I imagine being drunk feels.

"Um." I can barely think. Why had I come?

She shivers and pulls me into the entryway, then closes the door.

"I'd invite you in, but I'm not supposed to have people over when my parents are gone. So why are you here? Can't this wait until our meeting on Monday?"

Her shirt is white except for a large, yellow target in the middle. Yellow, her favorite color. The color of her voice. The middle of the target centers on a spot that I estimate is her belly button.

"Yeah, well, the thing is . . . I can't make the meeting. I have detention. For a week."

"A whole week? I wanted to start filming *this* week."

"I'm really sorry. I had this misunderstanding with some seniors . . ."

"Hold on. Maybe I can get Mr. Shaw to count our movie as extra credit for English. I mean, I am tutoring you for free. He's pretty cool about that kind of stuff. I can get him to bail you out of detention."

"Get me out of detention?" She would do that for me?

"Of course. We can't have the next Scorsese stuck in

detention when he's supposed to be making great movies, can we? I mean, our project won't work without you, Baxter. We need everyone involved in this and . . ."

I lean closer and find my lips pressed against hers. It isn't a matter of courage—I'd never have the guts to do it if I thought for a second about what I was doing. I don't have a choice in the matter. Her daffodil voice is too strong, and I can think of nothing but kissing her, a deep urgency that overtakes me and won't let go until my lips have touched hers.

As soon as I do it, though, I feel bewildered, like someone else is in control of my actions. I'm kissing Halle, who is beautiful and smart and confident and interesting and everything that I'm not. I have no right to be kissing her, but I can't stop. Her lips are soft and moist and she smells of lavender and tastes like strawberries. It's only when she leans into me, into the kiss, that I feel lightheaded and I drop my copy of *Gatsby* on the floor.

She pulls back then. I take in a deep breath, afraid I'll pass out from the sheer idea of what I've just done. I stand with my arms down at my sides, my head still swimming as I stare into her eyes for a hint of what she's thinking. She's everything to me, the girl I've loved since kindergarten. But right now I feel like a bug under her shoe. One harsh word will crush me in a hundred pieces.

What have I gotten myself into?

A Voice Full of Money

Her eyes smile at me. "That was unexpected," she says, "but nice. Where'd you learn to kiss?"

I can barely think. I still taste the strawberries on my lips. "The movies."

"You mean I'm the first?"

I flinch. I so hadn't wanted her to know that.

"That's so sweet."

No, that's so lame, but I can't lie to her now.

She bends down and picks up the book.

"Is this why you came over? You finished reading it?"

I nod weakly.

"Oh," she says and tilts her head. "I know. Don't you just love this book? I mean, it has everything; romance, mystery, the temptations of wealth, the importance of honesty, and the struggle to escape the past. Plus Jay Gatsby is my favorite scoundrel."

I look around the spacious foyer with marbled floors and think of Gatsby's mansion, and then I remember why I came in the first place. I remember what Gatsby said about Daisy, that "her voice is full of money." Is that what I hear in Halle's voice? Are the daffodils just an illusion?

"He's not a scoundrel. He's a victim," I insist.

Halle makes a *tsk* sound and rolls her eyes. "Gatsby not a scoundrel? Believe me, I know a lot about them. My father is one. People think he's some sort of hero around here because he employs so many people. But he doesn't really care about anyone except himself. It's the same with Gatsby. Everything he did was fake."

"His love wasn't fake. He cared about Daisy."

"Did he? Wasn't she just part of the plan? I mean, did he really even know her? She was more of an idea, a girl he romanticized. And years later, he didn't want to admit that she'd changed, that she was someone else entirely."

"How can you say that? He judged everything he had through her eyes. He bought a house across the bay from her. He never stopped loving her," I say, even though my throat constricts. I want to get it out, to tell her. "You can love someone for an eternity. Even someone you met in kindergarten."

She lets out a small laugh. "Isn't that stretching it a bit? You might have a crush in kindergarten. But fall in love?"

"Why can't you meet your soul mate in kindergarten?"

She reaches up and kisses me on the cheek. "You're a

hopeless romantic, Baxter. But no one meets their soul mate in kindergarten."

I look into her eyes, wishing I could reach inside and ignite the memories of how we once were. Inseparable. Living to see each other every day. "Are you sure about that?"

Something registers in her eyes, but she frowns, as though she doesn't trust the memory. "I barely even remember kindergarten."

My voice trembles. "What do you remember? From kindergarten?"

"Not much. I had a crush on a boy. He could recite entire movies. But I think I was his only friend. He was kind of weird."

I stand there, frozen by what she just said. My voice quivers. "That's what you remember?"

"I was five. It was so long ago. I can't even remember his name."

My head is spinning. "This is bullshit!" Suddenly, I have to get away. I turn and escape out the door. I hear Halle's voice calling me back, but I keep running.

Two blocks later I stop, out of breath, and kick at a large rock on the edge of the street. It strikes the curb and shoots back, hitting me in the shin. "Ouch! Damn it!" I look around. The street is dark and empty. I never swear; it reminds me too much of Dink. But I'm pissed. Did she know I was the boy from kindergarten? Was Halle messing with my head?

I wasn't as bad as she made me out to be. I had friends, other boys I played with. I just liked her better. Why did she think I was weird? Because I memorized movies? Because I was different from her?

A cool breeze rushes through my sweatshirt and I shiver and limp the rest of the way home. The memories flood my brain: how Halle volunteered to be my partner in every activity, how I'd tried to impress her by memorizing her favorite song, how she'd laughed at my impersonation of SpongeBob. I'd thought she liked me. Was she just being nice because she felt sorry for me? Is that how she remembers it?

When I get home, I open the back door as quietly as possible, but the hinges squeak. I almost make it through the kitchen when Mom turns on the light.

"Baxter! I thought you were asleep. It's almost midnight!"

"I know."

She shakes her head. "You'd better have a good explanation for being out this late."

Her hair is pulled back into a messy ponytail. She has sleep lines on her face. My best memory of Mom is when I was three and a half years old and she was painting. She'd pulled her long hair into a ponytail that day, too. But she was young and so pretty. She'd taken off my pants and let me walk in pie pans filled with paint. Then I'd walked across a large white canvas. Mom put on my favorite song: "John Jacob Jingle-heimer Schmidt," which started out slow but kept getting faster and faster. Soon I was jumping and hopping and dancing across the canvas, leaving messy footprints in my wake. Mom joined me and we both danced around the canvas, laughing until we fell down. It was before I'd realized that I was different from everyone else; an anomaly like the horse with two heads that Halle drew in kindergarten.

"Mom, am I really strange?"

"Where did this come from? And how does it have anything to do with you being out at midnight?"

"There was this girl in kindergarten. She was my best friend. At least I thought she was. Maybe she was just feeling sorry for me because I was strange and didn't have any other friends."

Mom sighs and sits down at the table. "No, that wasn't it. Sit down, Baxter."

I sit opposite her and fiddle with the salt shaker on the table. Mom has always been straight-up with me. Even when Dad died, she didn't sugarcoat it and say he fell asleep or was up in the sky watching over me.

Mom stares at my hands for a moment, then looks me in the eye. "I know you have an amazing memory, but you still remember people and incidents through your own perceptions. There was a little girl in kindergarten you had the hugest crush on. Her name was Hayley or something like that. You talked about her nonstop. And you followed her around like a lost puppy."

So far my memory seems accurate. That's the way I remember it, too. "It was Halle."

Mom puts her hand on mine. "Right. But she was the one who was different."

I pull my hand out from under hers. "No, she wasn't."

"Yes, she was. Halle was the one who didn't have any friends. The teacher told me that until you became her friend, she spent all her time alone in a little cardboard castle. She wouldn't come out the entire day. You were the only one who could coax her out."

"I would have known that."

"But you didn't. You saw what you wanted to see. What you needed to see."

"No!" My chest feels tight, like my breath is trapped inside. I remember everything, every detail. I would have known if Halle had social problems.

"It's okay, Baxter. That doesn't make your memory of her less valid. When she moved, you were heartbroken. But a month after, her mother called me. She said Halle missed you so much that she would barely eat, and she hadn't made any other friends at her new school. She was lost without you. You, on the other hand, had made friends with another boy in your class, and even though you missed Halle, you were happy."

"Why didn't you ever tell me?"

"Because I didn't want to upset you. You were adjusting well, at least better than Halle."

So my memory has limitations, just like everyone else's. I let it sink in, the imperfection, the messiness of it. All the memories of Halle change in this new view of her. I followed her around, but I was the one who got her to go outside to the playground. I was the one who volunteered to be Halle's partner, not the other way around. I was the one who initiated the game of tag in which our whole class joined. The data shifts and makes new connections. I can almost feel it moving around inside my head.

I let out a long sigh. I'd always assumed that my memories were correct. I hadn't thought of the fact that they might be tainted by my own perspective. What other memories were flawed?

"I guess my memory isn't perfect after all," I say.

She reaches over and squeezes my hand. "No one's is."

"But . . . I thought mine was."

"When it comes to facts, maybe. But when it comes to feelings, you can only see things through your own eyes. I certainly learned that lesson with Dink. Why are you thinking about that little girl now, after all these years?"

"Because there's this girl I really like at school."

Mom's face lights up. "That's wonderful, Baxter."

Yeah. Too bad she's the same girl. "So, I'm not too weird to have a girlfriend?"

"Do you know when I first realized you had an amazing memory?"

I shake my head. Mom never told me before.

"It was when you were five years old, two years after Dad died. I was looking at pictures of him because the anniversary of his death was coming up. I didn't think you remembered him because you were so young when he died, even though I showed you pictures all the time. And you asked me why I was so sad, and I said, 'Because I miss Daddy and I'm afraid I'm forgetting him.' And you said, 'Daddy had a laugh like an escalator.' And then you told me exactly what he said the day we went to the zoo, about how he told me I had a laugh like a hyena. I was shocked, but oh, so comforted. You gave him back to me for a few minutes more."

I remembered telling her about Dad. I just didn't know that it was so significant.

Mom has a wistful look in her eyes. "So even though I know your almost perfect memory sometimes feels like a curse to you, it's also a wonderful gift. Remember that. You've always seemed perfect to me."

The Truth about Hay

I'm up to my shoulders in hay bales, trying to lift one from the top of a stack that's almost as tall as I am. Brad throws them down like empty boxes. I'm getting stronger; I've already moved twice as many today as I did my first few days on the job. Pretty good, considering how tired I am. I barely dragged myself out of bed at seven this morning.

"We're stopping at noon today. Alexis is visiting her dad this weekend."

"Thank God for Alexis," I say, because I don't think I can last the whole day. I'm trying to work through the burn, but each bale feels heavier than the last one.

Brad laughs. "You can thank her in person. She's stopping over later."

Whenever I picture Brad's girlfriend in my head, she's always big. Maybe it's because Brad is such a big guy himself; not fat, but broad, like a younger version of his dad. But for all I know Alexis could be really cute.

As much as I want to quit working and go take a nap, part of me likes hauling bales of hay. It's simple work that doesn't require any thinking. I can empty my mind the same way I did when I rode my bike in California. The physical exertion required makes it difficult for the flashbacks to interfere.

"How's it going with Halle?" Brad asks.

"Okay." I'm worried that I might have screwed things up with her last night when I ran away. But I haven't called her yet. I don't know what to say. I don't have an excuse for what I did.

"You two seem pretty chummy around school."

"I kissed her." I don't mean to tell him; it blurts out on its own. Maybe it's because I can't stop thinking about the kiss. This is a memory I could play over and over for the rest of my life. I lick my lips and I can still taste the strawberries.

Brad reaches a gloved hand my way and gives me a high five. "Way to go. There's hope for you yet."

"Thanks." I feel my face flush and I turn away.

"I've known Halle since we were in grade school," he says. "She's always been nice to me, but I figured she'd hang with the popular crowd. I mean, coming from that kind of money? She's got more wardrobe changes than a model. But she was really shy in elementary school."

I take a swig from my water bottle. "I don't think she belongs here, to be honest." Maybe it's because I know her from California.

Brad nods. "It's harder to be rich on the Range than to be

poor. Makes a person stand out too much. Plus, she's a pack-sacker."

"A what?"

"Packsacker. An outsider. She wasn't born on the Range."

It strikes me how much this community is tied to the land, how they've had this connection since iron ore was discovered in the 1800s, and even before that when Native Americans lived off the lakes and forests. It's a vague, hard-to-understand connection, where they brag about the man-made bluffs and deep pits created by mining companies, but complain about how those same companies used them for cheap labor and compromised their health. And Halle is the perfect symbol of the enigma: she protests the very company that feeds and clothes her.

"I guess I'm a packsacker too, then."

"No. You're more like a tourist."

Brad turns to pick up another bale when his brother Karl grabs him from behind and pulls him to the ground. It takes a second before I realize they're just wrestling the way brothers do. They roll around in the dirt, their faces red from the exertion.

"Say mercy," Karl demands as he pushes Brad's shoulder into the ground.

"Forget it," Brad grunts.

Their clothes are caked with hay and leaves and dirt, but they're single-minded in proving their strength. I can't tell if Brad is mad or not. Even though Karl is older, Brad has twenty pounds and a few inches on him, and he manages to flip Karl over. But Karl is crafty and knows where to apply pressure to make Brad flinch, and pretty soon Karl is back on top. I have to move away when they roll in my direction.

Then Brad whispers something in his brother's ear. I don't hear what he says, but a moment later they're both jumping on me, and then we're all three on the ground, rolling in a bed of hay and dirt, flailing arms and legs and huffing breaths in the brisk air that smells like pine and manure and freshly mown grass. I'm no match for either of them, but it feels good to strain and grunt for the fun of it, to pit my strength, however lacking, against theirs. All the biking I did made my legs strong, but I don't have the upper-body muscle that they do.

We're still rolling around when Brad's mom comes out of the house with a petite girl whose blond hair bounces behind her in a ponytail.

"If you've got so much energy that you need to wrestle it off, then you're not working hard enough," Brad's mom yells, but there's a smile at the corners of her mouth.

We get up and Brad looks appropriately shame-faced in front of his girlfriend. Alexis reaches and runs a hand through his hair, brushing out stalks and chunks of dirt. She's nice-looking in a plain way, meaning that if she stood in a line with the other girls at my school I wouldn't be able to pick her out. But she has a kind smile and Brad can't take his eyes off her.

Brad's mom turns to leave. "Don't try to change him, Alexis. You'll just get frustrated. And Karl, what are you doing down here when you're supposed to be up in the loft?"

He puts his hands out. "There weren't any bales coming in. I figured they were quitting."

"Nobody's quitting till this rack's unloaded."

She goes back into the house. I know that when we're done she'll have a casserole and homemade bread and dessert waiting for us. Brad's dad will be there, too, and we'll sit around a long, oval table where the conversation will flow like water and I'll think *this is what a real family looks like*, because that's what I thought last time, and then I'll remember my dad again and feel sad.

Brad puts a gloved hand around his girlfriend's waist. "Hey, Alexis, meet the new kid at school, Baxter."

"Hi, Baxter." She gives a friendly wave. "Hey, Karl."

"Alexis," Karl says, stretching out the word. "Can't you find anyone better in the big city than this clod?" He pokes Brad, and a moment later they're back wrestling on the ground.

"Hi, Alexis," I say. And just so I don't feel awkward standing around watching the two of them wrestle, I drop down onto the dirt and join them.

Through the Camera Lens

"You have to be willing to experiment, especially with the lighting." Bob puts the camera on my shoulder. "See how it looks when you point at the window."

I peer through the lens and nod. Just because I memorized the instructions and functions doesn't mean it will translate into an ability to take good shots. The manual is filled with information about recording in different lighting conditions and using the manual controls, but I've never actually held a camera before. I've never noticed the way the sun casts a shadow across the wall or how artificial light is different from the natural kind, especially this early morning haze that holds a hint of orange as it cuts through the glass.

"Now point it at the corner, away from the light."

I aim the camera at the darkened corner of the classroom.

"So I need to set the white balance every time I film in a different location or lighting condition?"

"Exactly. Have you had any experience with this camera before?"

"Kind of," I say, and the lie slips off my tongue without much effort. I adjust the camera on my shoulder. It's heavier than I thought it would be. I'd fiddled with the camera on the tripod, but Bob wants me to get the feel of holding it in case I have to move around while filming.

Bob nods and folds his arms. He has on jeans and a flannel shirt, and even though he's older and has thick glasses, he tells us to call him by his first name instead of Mr. Schraan. "I thought so. I mean, most kids get confused with the scan reverse option. You're the first one who's understood it without my having to explain it ten times."

Eddie looks up from the thick manual he's reading. "I'm impressed, New Kid."

I aim the camera at Eddie and fiddle with the setting. Bob has been teaching me about framing subjects, about not leaving a lot of space above heads, about shooting from an angle and keeping the camera steady. I'm starting to get the hang of things and it makes me want to learn more. I like the way the world looks through the lens, how I can adjust a setting and create a different view of the subject. I seem to have a knack for it, too.

Eddie looks up and scowls, so I turn the camera toward the front of the room and center the clock in the frame, zooming in until I can see the dust particles on the top of the rounded glass. The clock is three minutes slow.

I want to focus on more people, but it's just the three of us in the room and Eddie clearly doesn't want the camera on him. He's a hard one to figure out. He's got this tough guy attitude, but he hangs around with a bunch of freshmen who can't even drive. He belongs to the Environmental Club, which is about as low on the social totem pole as you can get at Madison High; he doesn't seem at all concerned about what people think.

I'm tempted to record him so I can watch it later. How much does the camera capture? Can it reveal the idiosyncrasies behind his careful expressions? What about myself? Maybe my own memories are the result of an incorrect setting on the camera inside my head. I had it completely wrong in regards to Halle. If only I could adjust that internal lens as easily as the camera's.

Bob holds out a rectangular lens. "Will you be doing any wide-screen cinematic shots?"

"It'd be cool to have a wide-angle shot of the taconite plant," Eddie says.

Bob shakes his bald head. "Did you say the taconite plant? We don't normally let this equipment out of the school. It's too costly to replace."

"This is for our club project," Eddie says. "We need that footage."

"Well, I might do it for you, Eddie, if you take full responsibility and promise to return it in perfect condition."

Eddie puts up his hand. "You have my sacred vow as head of the prestigious Environmental Club."

"I'm going to need a signature to go along with that vow."

I place the camera in the bag. "We'll take good care of it."

Bob has Eddie sign out the camera. "It has a ninety-minute card in it. That should be plenty for a short video. There's another card in the side pocket if you run out."

Bob hands me the camera bag, and I put it over my shoulder. "Any more questions about how to use this? You already seem like a pro."

"He does, doesn't he?" says Eddie. He gives me an appraising nod. "You're full of surprises. I didn't think you knew anything about cameras."

I have to look away. "I read the manual. I'm a quick learner." I try not to sound too confident.

As we leave, Eddie mutters, "I just signed my life away. You better not screw up."

I wonder if I already have. Eddie's more suspicious than ever.

Monsters and Memories

"Halle, we're going to save you till last. We'll film you in front of the plant," Eddie says. He leaves to set up the background for Gina and Roxie on the opposite side of the classroom.

She looks up from the script she's working on. I haven't spoken to her since I ran away the other night. I search her eyes for anger or revulsion, or worse yet, pity. Has she figured out that I'm the boy from kindergarten?

"Thanks for getting me out of detention," I say politely. The fact that Halle has talked Mr. Shaw into excusing me to work on the video is mind boggling. I've never had much success in talking to teachers, much less getting special allowances from them.

I should say something about the other night, apologize

for running off. But part of me is still upset about Halle's comments about kindergarten, about her memory of that time. She was the one who was different, the one who had no social skills. She had it so wrong. Of course, so did I.

"This isn't going to work," she says, and a small wrinkle forms between her brows.

My stomach drops. I think of her lips, so soft and moist, of the smile she flashes so easily but which seems so fragile. I remember how it feels to be near her. I couldn't stand it if she rejected me now that I've experienced all that.

"It's all wrong," she says. "A video isn't going to do anything unless we get some hard evidence against Wellington Mines."

I take an appreciative breath and let it out. "What kind of evidence?"

"I don't know. Roxie has been looking into the rates of sickness in our area. We have that. But we don't have the employment histories of workers who later died of mesothelioma."

"How would you get that?"

She bites down on her lip. "I'm not sure. But we'll get it somehow. We're the good guys and the good guys always win. Right?"

She looks up at me innocently, as though she really believes this is true.

"It's true in the movies." I hold up the camera. "And this is a movie."

She smiles that fragile smile and studies me a moment. "Maybe after we drive out to the plant and you film me, I'll let you kiss me again. If you promise not to run away. You did like it, didn't you? You didn't leave because I'm a terrible kisser?"

My heart quickens at the thought of kissing her again. "No. Not at all."

"Good." She seems satisfied, but it lasts only a moment. "Why *did* you run away?"

I look down, preparing to tell another lie. Maybe a half truth. "I was angry at how *The Great Gatsby* ended. I wanted a happy ending."

Halle shakes her head. "Happy endings are reserved for fairy tales. *The Great Gatsby* isn't a fairy tale."

I set down the camera. "I disagree. It was a fairy tale, one with a tragic twist."

"I guess Gatsby could be seen as a kind of Prince Charming. He certainly thought of himself that way. He wanted to swoop down like a knight in shining armor and rescue his Princess Daisy. He just forgot to ask whether she wanted to be rescued."

"And she didn't?"

Halle sighs. "Some girls want to be rescued. I just think it was too late for Daisy."

Does Halle want to be rescued? What would it take to become her knight? A shiny new car? No, I doubt that would impress her. Halle isn't like Daisy that way. Even though she dresses in expensive clothing, she doesn't seem overly concerned about material goods. What if I could produce some incriminating evidence against Wellington Mines? Will that be enough to remove any chinks in the armor, the ones she's bound to find out about?

Halle goes back to studying the script she's working on, crossing out words and writing new ones in red above them. Knowing what I now know about her changes things. It makes sense, her being part of this rag-tag group instead of hanging around with the popular girls, even if she is drop-dead gorgeous and rich. She never felt comfortable in large groups— at least, she didn't in kindergarten. She was too shy and thoughtful.

Halle stops working after a moment and looks up at me.

"Mrs. Skrove."

I freeze. "What?" It sounds more like a croak.

"It's been bugging me since that night. I couldn't remember my teacher's name from kindergarten. I just remembered it. And that boy, his name was . . ."

I pick up the camera and point it toward the whiteboard. I wait for her to say my name, to make the connection in her brain, to realize who I am. I can't breathe. I can't look at her. The seconds tick by; the board blurs into a white screen and kindergarten at Pascal Elementary plays out before me.

"You be the monster," Halle insisted, taking her place behind the castle door.

"I don't want to be a monster. I want to be a fireman." I was wearing a red plastic fireman hat. "Monsters don't wear red hats," I said.

"Okay. Then you be a fireman monster."

"No."

"Then I'm not playing with you," she said from behind the door.

It was our first fight.

"There's no such thing as fireman monsters," I insisted, but she was silent behind the door. Finally, I went off to play with Ben, who was building a tower of Legos. Halle stayed in the castle the rest of the period. She peeked out at us. I saw one yellow pigtail hanging out from an opening and it reminded me of the story of Rapunzel, so I went up and pulled on the ponytail. Halle screamed. I felt bad and tried to say sorry but she was mad at me the rest of the day.

Maybe Halle has always thought of me as a monster. As much as I wish she'd remember me, I don't want her to see me that way.

Dr. Anderson said that most of the information people learn in life remains in their memories; they just can't recall it. Part of his research deals with the retrieval and storage length of memories, and how to restore them, or at least make them accessible. When I asked him what it's like to forget and try to remember, he said, "It's like losing something in your brain; you search every room trying to find it until you either get too tired of looking or it pops up in an unexpected place—for instance, between the sofa cushions of your cerebral cortex."

It made sense. The spot between the sofa cushions was where Mom always lost the remote for the television.

I peek from behind the camera. Halle sighs. "I usually have such a good memory. But I guess kindergarten *was* a long time ago." Her voice is troubled, as though the daffodils are being trampled under a heavy boot.

Gina comes up behind her. "Who remembers kindergarten? I barely remember last year."

"Okay, Baxter, we're ready for you," Eddie calls.

I breathe again. The shutter is now closed and I peer into the darkness of the camera, wishing I could empty my head and store my own memories inside that dark space.

Sharing Secrets

Halle's head is framed by the smoke-spewing stacks of the factory. I zoom out and she becomes a miniature-doll version of herself in her short leather coat with the fur-lined collar. The dark brown fur looks like a fake extension of her peanut butter–colored hair. I zoom back in until I can see the dimple in her chin. She licks her lips twice. I'll edit that out later.

Eddie waits until the noise of a passing truck fades away along with the dust left in its wake, then motions for her to start. She nods and blinks at the camera. "I live in the town that taconite built. It's all I remember growing up. Like everyone else here, I never questioned the safety of taconite processing. Until my grandpa got sick. He had mesothelioma, a rare form of cancer that's known to be caused by asbestos. Grandpa had worked in the plant for over forty years. Lots of people who worked at the plant started getting sick and dying of that same cancer. Last year, Grandpa died, too. If he were here, he'd say it's a trade-off, like the mining dust that used to get in people's lungs years before. He'd say it's the way of life on the Iron Range. Just part of the industry, just . . ." Her voice breaks. She pauses and gulps a breath of air. "But it doesn't have to be. People don't have to die to make a living. We deserve to have safe places to live and work. If things don't change, then someday we'll be known as the town that taconite killed."

She looks down. "That was terrible. I want to do it again. I can do it better."

My voice is soft. "No. It was perfect."

"Yeah," Eddie agrees. "Don't change a thing."

When Halle looks up, her eyes are wet. "What if this doesn't make a difference?"

I stop filming and put down the camera. A hawk flies overhead and lands on the high metal fence surrounding the plant. Across from it are thick trees filled with wildlife, dense forests, and lakes. They're unlikely neighbors. Down the road is a flattened animal, roadkill from the trucks that carry tons of rock. The hawk flaps its wings and I feel compelled to speak. "Sometimes a single voice can make a difference."

"It's a nice metaphor, but that's all it is," she says, sounding annoyed.

"I'm one person, one single voice. I testified against my mom's boyfriend. He went to prison because of me."

Halle stares at me, her face blank.

"You're screwing with us." Eddie's voice is unbelieving.

I keep my eyes on Halle. "No. It's true. That's why we moved here."

"So, are you saying you're in the witness protection program?" Eddie asks.

"No, nothing like that. He was released from prison a few months ago, and we didn't want him in our lives again. We wanted to get away. Far away." It feels right to tell them this, to share a real part of my life, one of the true parts. I wait for Halle to say something.

Her lips turn up at the corners. "Well, that explains a lot. No one in his right mind would move here unless he was hiding out."

Eddie glances around as though he's being followed. "So what did this dude do? And is he the vengeful type?"

"He stole money from the clients at his workplace. And yes, he wants revenge because I testified against him. He wants to find me and break my legs, or worse. I don't think he's looking in Minnesota, though. We don't have any ties to this place."

Halle's eyes widen. "The plot thickens. A mysterious past and the pursuit of a convicted felon. Ooh, I love it. What's the jerk's name?"

"His name's Dink."

She makes a shivering motion. "Even his name is disgusting." She takes my arm. "We'll have to keep a close eye on you. Maybe fit you with a disguise. Dye your hair blond or get a fake mustache."

Is she making fun of me? Does she believe my story?

Halle cocks her head. "Hey, Eddie, do you think Baxter is ready for a tour of a haunted mine?"

Eddie raises his eyebrows. "If he's looking to hide, that's the perfect place."

Okay, so maybe they don't believe me. It doesn't matter. Some of the weight of my secret has been lifted. I can breathe easier, and Dink doesn't seem quite so scary now. I hold up the camera, ready to play along. "Maybe we can put it in our video."

• • •

Halle's brown eyes grow dark and her voice takes on a foreboding tone. "Jasper Campbell was his name. He died along with nine others when the mine was flooded. Turns out it was too close to the lake. Jasper could have climbed out and lived, but he stayed behind to pull the warning whistle so other miners could get away. The warning whistle continued to blow for days after he died, until they finally cut the rope. They had to drain the lake in order to find the bodies. Took them nine months. They say you can still hear the whistle blow at the same time that it flooded."

We'd followed a narrow trail across rolling hills through a forested area of crunchy leaves. My legs are sore and a cold wind whips through my jacket. I wished I'd dressed warmer. Plus I have to worry about the camera. If I drop it, I'll have more than Dink to contend with.

And now this. A small plaque. I expected more. It lists the names of the dead. The lake is visible through a curtain of maple and aspen trees, a pristine waterway that juts to the right. Waves slap eagerly at the shore as though awaiting more victims.

Eddie rubs his hands together. He has on a light jean jacket. No one seems to dress for the cold here. They just endure it.

"It's not just the whistle. When they tried to reopen the mine, the first miners down there saw the decaying body of Jasper Campbell with the rope still tied to his waist. They left and never went back, and the mine closed down for good."

"This is it? Where's the mine?" I look down at the iron plaque. If they're trying to scare me, they could at least bring me to some spooky ruins.

Eddie points at the lake. "It's under there. When they closed the local mines and stopped pumping the lakes, nature reclaimed the area."

I imagine trout and walleye swimming through the submerged mine shafts and rotting wood. Okay, that's a bit scarier, but it's nothing compared to Dink's gargoyle tattoo. And it's actually kind of scenic here. The bright blue of the lake is set against a background of yellow, orange, and red forest. Cattails line the east side of the lake, their cigar-shaped ends waving in the breeze. I've never seen anything so beautiful. We're surrounded by a picture from a postcard.

"But there's more." Halle motions for me to follow her. She leads me away from the plaque around a row of tall pine trees where the terrain juts up against a rocky hill.

"Back here." She pulls at some vines and shrubs to reveal a deep hole in the hill. "We found some rusty equipment in here; wooden logs and old axes and shovels and pieces of iron ore."

I peer into the darkness of the hole. It's barely big enough for one person to crawl through. "How far back does it go?"

Eddie takes a flashlight from his pocket and waves it in the opening. "Drops down suddenly about twenty feet in. Probably led down to the shafts, but it's full of water now, too."

Halle pushes at my back. "Go on. Don't be scared. You won't fall down a rabbit hole. Just a mine shaft."

I stiffen. "I'm not scared. I just don't want to break the camera."

"Then leave it out here and go in. I'm right behind you."

Part of me wonders if they're playing a trick on me. Are they going to do something like put a rock in front of the hole after I crawl in, just to scare me? I don't want Halle to think I'm a coward, so I set the camera in the grass and crawl through leaves and tree branches and rocks, cautiously moving my hands along the cold ground. Who knows what creatures are living in here now?

I'm relieved when I hear Halle right on my heels. "This is so exciting," she coos. "This place always gives me goose bumps."

Somehow, with her behind me it doesn't seem so bad. If Eddie weren't here, it would almost be romantic. Our own make-out mine shaft.

I stop not far inside. The small entrance expands into a tall tunnel. I stand up and wipe at the rust stains on my jeans. It's the color of the landscape: birches and pines and red earth.

Eddie flicks his flashlight toward the far end of the tunnel where pieces of wood are nailed together in the shape of an X, like a railroad crossing post. I can hear the distant sound of water gurgling in a hole beyond the wood.

"This was part of the mine?" I ask.

"We think so. We haven't told anyone else about it."

We sit on wooden logs. An old helmet fitted with a half-burned candle sits by my feet.

Halle grabs the flashlight from Eddie and aims it at her

face. "The only people who know about this place are Eddie and me and Gina and Roxie. And now you. So you have to make a solemn vow never to reveal this location to anyone else."

"Shouldn't you have made him promise that before you showed him where it is?" asks Eddie.

She shrugs and shines the light on my face. "He'll never remember how to find this place anyway. So, what do you say, Baxter?"

She never showed Hunter. It makes me feel all warm inside, even though my hands are frozen. I squint in the light. "I promise."

Halle waves the flashlight back and forth in front of my eyes. "You can use this place for your special hiding spot, in case you need to get away from Duke."

"Dink," I say.

"Right. Whatever. But first you must undertake a very important task to show your commitment to the Mental Club."

I haven't felt this way since kindergarten, when Halle and I pretended we were the king and queen of the castle and tried to keep everyone else out.

I'm ready to take on the world. Even Dink doesn't scare me as much now. Somehow, telling people about him makes him less of a threat. I've never felt so happy to be in a cold hole in blustery Minnesota. "What do I have to do?"

How to Spend $65,358.97

Editing a video is more difficult than I thought it would be. It requires creativity, which has never been part of my vocabulary.

Luckily, Eddie has a vision.

"I brought music to overlay the video. A ballad that's guaranteed to pull on the heartstrings," he says. "It makes my mom cry whenever she listens to it."

Pictures of the deceased flash across the screen against the stark background of the plant that we'd filmed earlier. Bob helps us, explaining how to combine live action, still pictures, and blank screen with writing on it. I even take notes, and keep them next to me so Eddie can see me checking them from time to time.

While I'm fake-looking at the notes, I think about how someday science will find a way to manipulate memory, to download or upload experiences that we want to remember or forget, just like editing a movie in our brains. The first thing I'll do then is erase every trace of Dink. I'll erase the gargoyle tattoo and the Winston cigarettes that made him smell like a walking chimney, and then the fake smile he flashed like he really cared about you.

I hate that he gets in my head when I'm trying not to think about him. I hate remembering him at all.

"I'll pick you up again tomorrow on the way to school," Eddie offers, his voice sounding almost friendly. I'm finally beginning to feel like part of the club. I almost look forward to the secret task Halle has planned for me.

• • •

"So, do you know why I'm supposed to go to the football game on Saturday, and what Halle wants me to do?" I ask as we're copying the video onto a DVD. It's 7:38 a.m., the third day in a row that I've come in early. I stayed late once, too. But Eddie has spent even more time on it, skipping lunch and study hall and an occasional class.

Eddie smirks. "Of course I do. You don't think she's the only mastermind in our group, do you? We all like a good prank."

A prank? The hair on my neck bristles. "What kind of prank?"

"The only kind there is: the kick-ass, hair-raising kind."

I put the DVD in my backpack and try not to show my anxiousness.

He notices anyway. "Don't worry about it," he says. "The Mental Club takes care of its own."

Eddie says "its own" like I'm part of the club, part of the group. It's the first nice thing he has ever said to me.

"You're the only senior in the club. What will happen next year without you?"

"Halle's the heart and soul of the club. Besides, I'll still be hanging around. Gina and I, well, I think we're in it for the long haul."

"You're not going to work at the plant, are you?"

Eddie forces a laugh. "No way. I know; there's not much else to do in town. It's the whole moral dilemma of this place: the taconite plant keeps this town going, but do the environmental concerns outweigh the benefits? We can't have both, so should we be happy to just have jobs?" He shakes his head. "I'm going to be the first one in my family *not* to work in the mine. Just because they bought into all that bull doesn't mean I have to."

"So are you going to leave?"

"They're not getting rid of me that easy. But working on this video made me think. There's a graphic design program at the community college in Hibbing. I might look into it."

I nod. "I can see you doing that."

"Thanks. I appreciate your hard work on this. I know it's not necessarily your thing."

"I'm beginning to understand it more," I say, because it's true. "We could add another interview if you want. I could tape you."

"We got enough sob stories. I don't want to overdo it."

"But your perspective would add something."

"Why? Because we need the Native American point of view?"

he says sarcastically. "You want to film me looking at the plant and then show a tear running down my face?"

"No. I meant that the other interviews were all girls. It'd be nice to have a guy's perspective."

"Oh."

"Sorry. You don't have to . . . I mean, it's private and all," I fumble with the words.

Eddie holds up a hand. "Take it easy. I'm the one who should apologize. I just didn't want to make it a cultural thing. I mean, we're talking about cancer. People want to ignore it. Look at the kids at this school. They don't give a rat's ass about our club because they think it can't happen to teenagers. But it can. It *has* happened . . ."

"To who?" Then it hits me. "You?"

Eddie scowls.

"You have cancer?"

"Had." He grimaces. "This is strictly confidential."

"Oh, yeah, I wouldn't . . . mesothelioma?"

"No. A different cancer. I was born with it, but we still think it was environmental because my mom worked at the plant." He taps the desk with his hand. "I've been cancer-free since I was four. So, no, I'll never work there. But my mom still does."

Eddie's anger makes sense now. "That has to suck." It's the only thing I can say.

"It does. But things could be worse. I could have a lunatic convict after me." He raises his eyebrows.

I nod. "Touché."

"You're okay to send the package?" Eddie asks.

"Priority mail," I confirm. I'll add the note that Roxie wrote imploring a study on the taconite mines and factories, along with case histories that she and Gina have put together. All in a padded envelope to the Institute of Natural Resources.

Bob comes out of his office. "You two should be proud. That video was better than I thought possible."

"Yeah. We did good, New Kid." Eddie gives me a slap on the back. Another compliment from Eddie. I shrug, not sure what it means, but it feels good for a change.

We walk down to the first floor, where we're showing an advance screening, a celebration of all our hard work. Halle's bringing snacks. I'd be more excited if I weren't still worried about the prank they're planning. Dink left me gun-shy about surprises.

A large screen covers the whiteboard and a row of chairs is set up in front.

Halle stands behind a table with the treats she brought: taconite cookies (chocolate-drop cookies in small round balls with chocolate frosting) and red punch.

"I made them myself," she says triumphantly, handing me a cookie. They're as hard as real taconite, but I smile and ask for seconds.

Eddie claps his hands. "Welcome to the world premiere of the Mental Club's first live-action movie. If I say so myself, it's worthy of an Oscar."

Halle sits next to me and leans in, like we're a couple and have been for a while. I sneak glances her way without being too conspicuous. I've tried to memorize Halle's face and failed. Not because I can't remember it, but because it changes every time I see her. There's always another line in her frown or a sparkle in her eyes that I haven't noticed before. I could spend a lifetime trying to memorize it.

The video ends with pictures of all the people who've died of mesothelioma. The words at the end emblazon the screen: **TACONITE KILLS!**

Roxie claps and wipes tears from her eyes. "It's great. It'll knock their socks off."

Gina lets out a hoot. "It looked like a real freakin' movie," she says. "We may have to change our name to something more elite than the Mental Club."

Halle nods and claps, but her smile is fixed and transparent. Something is wrong. She goes to pack up the refreshments. After I celebrate with the others I approach her. "What did you think?"

"It's a great video," she says, but her voice lacks its usual sparkle.

"You didn't like it."

"I love it, really I do," she insists. "I'm just afraid that it's not enough. My dad says that they've complied with all the regulations and have a good relationship with the Department of Health. When I confronted him with the list of names, he said they all had different jobs at the plant and the mine. And they could have been exposed to asbestos or some other chemicals at home or somewhere else."

She waves her hand. "I'm sorry. I don't mean to spoil the celebration. I'm just afraid for Eddie and Gina and Roxie, of getting their hopes up and having them squashed down. I'm afraid they'll give up, and it will be the end of everything; the club and the protests and . . ."

"I'll still be part of the club. I won't give up."

She gives me a kiss on the cheek. "That's because you're the real thing, Baxter." But her voice is sad.

I researched taconite production and I know there's no easy fix. When the pure iron ore ran out on the Iron Range, taconite became the next big thing, even though it had been considered a waste product before. The hard rock is broken up, ground into a powder, and the extracted ore is rolled into marble-sized pellets. It's dirty and dusty and hard for workers not to inhale the taconite fibers, which might cause meso-thelioma. But the old equipment at the plant, which has since been replaced, contained asbestos—and that also causes meso-thelioma.

When I get home from school I wonder what I can do to put the sparkle back in Halle's voice. She already has lots of nice clothes and she isn't into fancy cars or motorcycles. If I spend sixty-five thousand dollars on her, it has to be for some-thing special, something she wants more than anything else in the world.

I go to the closet and take the envelope out of the guitar case. How would Mom feel if she knew I had the money? How would Halle feel if she knew I was a thief?

The hundreds dangle like Monopoly money stuck beneath a game board. I played Monopoly with Dink once. Dink cheated.

I draw my fingers through the crisp bills. I can't tell anyone about the money; not Mom or Halle, or even Dr. Anderson. And if I can't tell anyone, then how can I spend it? What will they say if I buy something expensive? They'll wonder where I

got the money. It's a lose-lose situation. I have all this money
that I can't spend.

But no matter how scared I am, there's no way I'm giving
the money to Dink. I sit on the edge of my bed and kick off my
shoes. I take out the DVD and the letter Roxie wrote, along
with the three pages of case histories. I read them, all eighteen
of them, including Halle's grandfather. I read how he'd started
at a young age at the iron ore mines before they closed down,
and then transferred to the taconite mines, working his way
up to middle management. He said that mining was in his
blood; if you cut him, he'd bleed taconite. He'd fought the cancer for three years before he died. I read how he was Halle's best
friend, and how much she misses him every day.

I stop reading. That's who she's really afraid of losing. It's
not the club, really, or the protesting. Halle's grandfather is
the sparkle in her voice. I hear it whenever she talks about him.
I even hear it on the video when she mentions him.

Suddenly, I know what I'm going to do with the money.

Hunter's Move

Halle taps her fingernails on the wooden table, waiting. "So, how'd you do on the test?"

"Ta-da. B!" I show her the front of my test, with the words "Great Improvement" beneath the score.

Mrs. Algren makes a shushing sound from her desk. I nod in acknowledgment, but it's not like we're making as much noise as the group sitting on the other side of the library. Jenna White is there with two other girls. She blows her nose and lets out small sobs, which elicit waves of comfort from her tablemates.

Halle scrunches up her face. "Not bad. Although . . . I thought you'd ace that test."

I considered it, but going from a C-minus to an A seemed extreme. Plus, what if Mr. Shaw decided that I didn't need tutoring anymore? "Really, I'm happy with this grade. All thanks to you," I say.

She grabs the test out of my hand before I can stop her. "What'd you get wrong?"

I instinctively reach for the test.

She holds it away from me. "What? Can't your favorite tutor see your test results?"

"You're my only tutor."

"Which makes me your favorite."

"Can't argue with that logic."

My fingers itch while she looks at the test. I open and close them in a fist, fighting the urge to grab it away from her and stick it in my backpack.

"This is odd," Halle says, and my heart thumps. "The one easy part of the test, easy if you've read the book, anyway, is matching the quote with the character. You got most of those wrong." She shakes her head, as if she doesn't understand. But how can she? I needed to get a certain percentage wrong, and this was the easiest way to do it. It was either that or leave one of the essay questions blank.

"I ran out of time. I didn't even read them, to be honest. Just filled in the blanks." I sound as sincere as I can, considering that my heartbeat is pounding in my ears.

"Oh, well, that explains it." But she looks at me oddly.

I shrug and try not to disintegrate into the desk. "Next time I'll do better."

"Next time you'll ace it," Halle says.

My fifth-grade teacher flashes in my mind.

Miss Noll was a young teacher with long blond hair, and she acted like every fifth-grade boy had a crush on her, and half of us did, but she was always trying to be our friend instead of our teacher. When I memorized every town in California from a state map hanging in her room, she started telling everyone that I had a perfect memory. She said it to be nice, but it made me feel different. Up until then my teachers had always known I had a great memory, but they didn't make as much of it or expect me to be a performing robot. Miss Noll had me recite pages out loud after I'd read them. "You aced it. You're a genius!" she'd say and high-five me. Afterward, the rest of my class would make snide comments, like "Are you sure you're human?" Some of them started calling me Data from the Star Trek shows.

Hunter enters the library surrounded by his posse. He waves at Halle. This causes Jenna to erupt into renewed sobs at her table.

It also makes Hunter uncomfortable. He avoids eye contact with Jenna and stops in front of our table. "Say, Halle. I hear you're doing some tutoring." He looks at me and it's clear he thinks that's the only reason she's sitting with me. Like she wouldn't be sitting here otherwise. "I could use some help with math. You were a big help last year. I just wonder if you might make some time for me. I'm free tonight, if you want me to come to your house. Or you could come to mine."

"I'm not taking on more students right now. Maybe Jenna can tutor you."

Hunter flashes a brief look in Jenna's direction and squirms. "We broke up last night."

Halle looks at Jenna's table. "That explains a lot."

"I know you probably hate me, but I really do need a tutor. I'm willing to pay you," he offers. He sounds sincere and completely innocent, but I know he's not, because this is just what Brad warned me about.

"I already have plans with Baxter tonight. But you can join us to study at my house if you really want," she says all friendly-like, and I wonder if she's reconsidering his offer now that she knows Jenna's out of the way. Then it hits me. I've just been invited to Halle's house.

Hunter's face clouds over. I can tell he doesn't like the fact that I'll be there. "Yeah, well, at seven o'clock, then? Thanks," he says, then turns and leaves.

Halle grabs my hand. "You *have* to come to my house tonight. Say you will."

"I will." There's no way I'm leaving the two of them together.

She lets out an exaggerated breath. "Oh, thank you, Baxter."

"Why did you go out with him to begin with? He doesn't seem like your type."

"Oh, Hunter can turn on the charm when he wants. He helped me smash open the pop machine last year. Said I brought out the activist in him."

She shakes her head. "Don't you hate it when people act phony? He did that stuff, which he didn't really believe in, just to make me like him."

"So . . . you did like him," I say. I search her for the truth, but Halle's face is the only thing I *can't* memorize, and the truth remains elusive.

Halle reaches over and gives me a quick kiss on the lips. She smiles at me reassuringly.

"At one time I did. But I would have broken up with him eventually. We're just too different."

I tuck my test into my backpack. I'd object to that, but I don't want to make a case for Hunter. I want to believe that we're different, that I'm not like him at all. But the truth is that I'm doing the same thing he did. And he has more in common with Halle than I do. All I have is a few months of kindergarten memories tucked away like a movie in a corner of my mind. The Halle I knew was shy and scared and hid behind the walls of a cardboard castle. Somewhere in the years between then she's come out of her shell and become a brazen leader who speaks her mind and goes her own way without conforming to anyone else's standards.

I think of Daisy, of how Halle said she was a different woman than the one Gatsby fell in love with, and how he couldn't see that. Am I doing the same thing, following an idea of a girl I knew years ago?

Then why do I feel the way I do? Why can't I stop thinking about her? Why does every moment with her seem like the only time I'm really alive?

I want so much for Halle to know the real me, to like me for who I am. But I can't take the risk. I can't lose her. Maybe I was infatuated with Halle at five years old. But I'm hopelessly in love with her at fifteen.

Why It's Normal to Be Jealous

"**This is where** your tutor lives?" Mom's eyes pop when she pulls into the U-shaped driveway. "What do her parents do for a living?"

"Her dad works at the taconite plant." I get out before she can ask any more questions. My fear is that our six-year-old Corolla will stall before she makes it out of the driveway.

I'm early. My plan is to beat Hunter here. I don't want to find him cuddling up to Halle. I'd rather it be the reverse, but what I'm really hoping for is that Hunter doesn't show up at all.

Halle leads me down a hallway into a spacious kitchen that's roughly the size of our whole townhome. There's a two-tier island in the middle with a granite surface and padded bar stools. The custom cherry cabinetry rises up to ten-foot ceilings. A patio door leads out to a darkened three-season porch and deck. Halle directs me to a small table in a rounded area of the kitchen, what Mom would call a breakfast nook. "Hunter's not here yet. I thought we'd set up at the table. Make yourself comfortable and I'll go get my books. There's juice and bottled water in the fridge." She leaves me alone.

I set my backpack on the floor next to the table and take out my math book. It still bothers me that Halle invited Hunter to her house. Why didn't she just say no? Is it because she still has feelings for him?

Halle's dad walks into the kitchen. He doesn't see me at first. He opens the refrigerator and takes out a bottle of water. I make a small coughing noise.

He turns around. "Oh. I didn't know Halle had company."

I stand up and nod. "Hi. I'm Baxter."

Her dad comes over and shakes my hand, a firm but quick handshake. "Nice to meet you, Baxter." There's no hint of recognition. I don't think he knows I'm one of the protesters at the taconite plant. I wonder what he'd think of me if he knew how I spent the sixty-five thousand dollars.

He nods at my book. "Doing some studying?"

"Yes, sir. Halle's tutoring me."

"Tutoring? Well, I'm glad to see her spending her time wisely. I half expected you to be making protest banners."

"If Halle asked me to make them, I would," I blurt out. "I mean, I think it's admirable that she's concerned about the environment."

He lets out a small sigh. "It would be more admirable if she'd find someplace to protest besides the taconite plant. I'm afraid we don't see eye to eye on many things these days.

Sometimes I wish she was five again. She was a lot easier then. At least that's how I remember it."

"My mom says the same thing," I reply.

He smiles, and it sparks a memory:

"Don't leave me, Daddy!" It was the fourth day of school. Halle was crying and hugging her dad's leg. I was playing nearby with a blow-up dinosaur that was bigger than me. If I put it down, someone else would have grabbed it.

"I'll pick you up after school," he said patiently.

"Can I call you to come get me?" she asked tearfully.

"Sure, Halle. But your teacher has activities planned for you. You won't want to leave early."

"What's your phone number at work?" Halle asked.

Mrs. Skrove came over and took Halle's hand. "Do you want to play in the castle again?" she asked in a comforting voice.

Halle nodded but tugged on her dad's pant leg. "I need your number, Daddy."

He smiled and told her his number. "But I don't think you'll need to call me, sweetie. You're going to have so much fun. Daddy has to go now or he'll be late." He bent down and kissed her on the cheek.

Halle started to cry again. Mrs. Skrove nodded at Halle's dad to leave and led Halle to the castle. Halle eventually settled down.

Ten minutes later I saw Halle's dad at the door of our classroom, peeking in. He had an expression on his face where he was smiling but looked like he might cry at the same time. I stood to go get Halle, but her dad put his finger to his lips and shook his head at me.

I see that same expression on his face now.

"My wife is at a meeting, but let Halle know that I'll be in the den if she needs anything," he says, then leaves.

I help myself to a bottle of water from the massive steel refrigerator.

The doorbell rings and Halle's voice echoes in the hallway. "I've got it."

A minute later she comes into the kitchen, followed by Hunter.

Darn.

Hunter looks equally pleased to see me.

"Oh, hi," he says dismissively.

"Well, let's get to work, boys," Halle says, and she sits in between us and bends down to read the first problem. Hunter is a year older but he's taking the same math course as us. He moves his book close to hers and leans over so his face is almost touching her hair. He sniffs. The jerk is smelling her hair!

Brad was right. Hunter is making a move right in front of me, like I can't see what he's doing. I stretch my foot under the table and wrap it around Hunter's chair. Then I pull, using all those leg muscles I've built up from bike riding. Hunter's chair flips backward and he lands on the floor.

"What the . . . ?" he yells.

"Hunter!"

Halle's dad rushes out of his office. "What's that noise? What happened?"

"Um . . . sorry, Dad. Hunter was leaning back and his chair tipped." Halle helps Hunter up. He glares at me.

Halle's dad raises an eyebrow. "Be careful with the furniture, won't you, boys?"

"Yes, Mr. Phillips." Hunter's ears and neck are pink.

He waits until Halle's dad goes back into his office before

he gets in my face. "Your head is a hockey puck and I'm going to smash it to bits!"

Halle pulls on his arm. "Hunter, what are you doing?"

"Your psycho friend pushed my chair over."

"Really? Baxter? It's so unlike him. Are you sure you didn't just fall over?"

He straightens and picks up his books. "Let's try this another time, Halle. Give me a call when you get rid of this loser." He points at me. "You're roadkill."

I don't care what he calls me as long as he leaves.

Halle follows him to the door. I hear murmurs and it's all I can do not to follow them. When Halle returns, her arms are crossed. "Did you really flip Hunter's chair?"

I cross my arms. "Did you really expect the three of us to study together?"

"Some things look better on paper," she admits.

I confront her then. I don't want to be demanding, but it comes out sounding exactly that way. "Why did you really invite Hunter? Do you still like him?"

"Oh, God, no. I invited him because he really does have a hard time in math. Hunter told me he wants to turn pro, but he might play college hockey first. *If* he can get into college. It's his only way out of this town."

"There are other tutors besides you."

She sits down on my lap. "You're jealous? I don't usually find that to be an endearing trait, but it looks kind of cute on you."

Every single nerve in my body tingles. My anger melts and changes into a raging blob of excitement.

"He sniffed your hair," I say, even as I'm guilty of doing the same as she leans up against me.

Halle kisses me on the neck. "So I should be thanking you for protecting the honor of my tresses?"

I look at the door to her father's office. I feel guilty and scared and excited and I wish he wasn't just beyond that door.

Halle notices and whispers in my ear. "If my dad comes out and sees me here, he'll ground me for a month." She kisses my ear.

I kiss her then, because how can I resist? She kisses me back, a deep, sensual kiss that threatens to knock me out, and just when I think one of us has to breathe, the phone rings. Halle jumps off me and moves back to her own chair, where she busily writes down the next problem. I let out a ragged breath, feeling dizzy and hot, and I can barely see the words in front of me.

"By the way, thank you for knocking Hunter down," she says.

And she still doesn't look at me, but that's good because I'm sure I have the dumbest smile on my face.

A Pi Contest

"Does anyone know who Daniel Tammet is?"

Mr. Feege's eyes scan the room quickly as though he doesn't expect an answer.

I've been reliving last night with Halle, the hot and sultry kiss that made me dizzy. I'm hoping that I can find a way, through reliving that kiss, to keep from feeling faint next time. But the memory is so raw, so fresh, and so sensory, that I still feel light-headed when I think of it. It's made me feel invincible. When Hunter stuck out two fingers toward me from across the hallway to let me know he was planning something, I wanted to go up and shake his hand and thank him for leaving last night. If there's a heaven, I'm in it.

And now I'm going to see Halle tomorrow evening at the football game to perform a task that proves my loyalty, and I don't want to risk passing out and missing the best part—the kissing part, if there happens to be one, from the girl I love.

I rushed to school this morning to see Halle for a few minutes before class, and she gave me some leftover taconite cookies from her locker. She smelled like hairspray and fruity lotion and I inhaled deeply before leaving her. Then I saw Bob in the hallway and spoke to him before running to class. I never knew life could be this busy or this full. The last three years haven't prepared me at all. Before that, elementary school was so structured. But high school is a completely different life. So many opportunities. So much freedom.

Now I find my hand rising in the air of its own accord when the teacher asks about Daniel Tammet. My voice comes from inside, from that place where you answer when you're sort of paying attention, but not really focused. "He recited pi to 22,514 decimal places."

Mr. Feege's eyes widen. "That's right, Baxter."

Is it weird to know that fact, or normal? The class murmurs appreciatively. Maybe it's okay to know math trivia. Maybe it makes me sound cool. My voice takes courage in this and I go on.

"The record holder is Chao Lu from China, who recited pi to 67,890 decimal places on November 20, 2005, although another man, Akira Haraguchi, supposedly recited 100,000 digits in 2006, but it was unverified." I don't mention that Daniel Tammet is a high-functioning autistic savant. Okay, maybe that's a little over the top. Or way over.

I hate the giggling the worst. It always makes me feel like

they're trying not to laugh, but can't help it because I'm such a loser. I look down at my book, feeling their eyes on me.

"Excellent," Mr. Feege says.

But it's not excellent. It's careless. First the football team, then English, now math. Kids are looking at me differently. I wish I had a filter in my brain, one that would tell me when I'm revealing too much. I can't afford to get too comfortable in class or anywhere else, for that matter. Every moment with Halle is not only a chance to be near her, it's also an opportunity to mess up. She already remembered Mrs. Skrove's name. And then I confessed about Dink. What if she tries to look up Dink on the Internet? At least Dink is a nickname, one that wasn't used in news articles. And I didn't tell her Dink's last name. Chances are she'll have a hard time finding anything. But there's always the risk. The risk that I'll reveal too much. The risk that she'll remember me. Will it matter now?

"Baxter's abundance of information is a great segue into our class project," Mr. Feege says. "We're going to have our own pi contest."

The class moans in unison. Everyone except me, because I'm trying to melt into my desk, to become a blob of nothingness that can't raise its hand in class because blobs don't have hands.

"Hey, it's not that bad," Mr. Feege says. "It just takes a little mental preparation and memorization. My college professor used to say that you should be as smart as the instruments you're using."

"Looks like Baxter already is," says a voice behind me that

sounds like blackboard dust. It's Jeb Danner, the brother of Scott, aka the guy I pushed down in the hallway. Jeb already torments me in English, and when I turn around, he has the same sneer on his face as his brother had in the dean's office.

I want to tell Jeb to shove it because math is the one subject I have to work at. Math requires logic, and having a perfect memory doesn't make me smart or able to solve mathematical problems. Memorizing formulas doesn't mean I always use them correctly.

Of course, memorizing pi is another matter. I've never tried it before. I've only read about the men who memorized it because they had amazing memories, and I was searching for a connection. But there's no way I'll make the mistake of taking part in a pi contest. As much as I like school, I'm beginning to hate my classes; every minute is another opportunity to expose the real Baxter. I miss Dr. Anderson's vibrant voice, a calm port in the choppy sea of words and voices. Life was a lot easier in his lab. But as he often reminded me, I'm not a lab rat.

Mr. Feege holds up a finger. "I'm handing out a sheet that lists the pi digits to one thousand places. Of course, I don't expect you to memorize all thousand, but you should be able to do thirty to fifty, and if you use the mnemonic devices listed on the other side, you could do twice that many. I'm getting something good for a prize, so take this seriously, class."

The bell rings early for a pep rally in the gym. As I exit the room I'm pushed from behind and I fly out into the crowded hallway. Amazingly, this time I don't knock anyone down. I don't see who pushed me, but I hear Jeb laugh and yell, "Watch out for the flying nerd." Great. Time to show support for the jerks who want to slam me into the ground.

I'm following the crowd to the gym when Mr. Jackson's voice stops me. "Mr. Green."

I turn around to see him standing with his arms folded in the middle of the hallway. The flow of students makes a wide berth around him.

"You have an appointment with me on Monday. Twelve o'clock sharp. Don't forget."

We face each other like we're scheduled for a high noon showdown, except the only thing that's loaded is my memory. But I'm ready for him. I read the stupid rules.

I'd tip my hat if I were wearing one. I nod at him and join the swarm pouring into the gym. The band is playing a school anthem that sounds like every other school anthem. Cheerleaders wave their orange-and-black pom-poms and jump up and down. The first eight rows of the bleachers are taken by the football teams, in descending order from the ninth-grade team to the varsity team that fills the first two rows.

The last thing I need is to see football players. I hug the railing and hide behind other students until I reach the second level.

"Baxter," Halle calls from the upper stands. "Over here."

"Going to the game tomorrow night isn't a good idea," I say after I've squeezed past five people to sit next to her. "The whole football team wants to drop kick me."

"But I'll be there, and so will Gina and Roxie. Wouldn't you take on the whole football team just to be with me?"

"Well, maybe the JV team."

"I'm not into the whole sports thing, Baxter. *You* have to go to complete your very important task. I'm only there for emotional support."

"You still haven't told me anything about it. How am I supposed to complete it if I don't know what it is?"

"It's so top secret that we can only reveal it at the right moment, Baxter. At tomorrow night's football game."

"Is it something you've all done before, or did you conjure it up just for me?"

She puts her arm through mine. "We made it up for you. And no, Gina and Roxie never had to perform a special task, but that's because they were with me when I found the tunnel. And Eddie is our driver, so we can't make him do anything. But you're the first person who's ever seen the tunnel other than us, so you should have to do something to prove your loyalty. Besides, it will be fun and will promote the Mental Club's goals and ethics."

I try to imagine what kind of prank would promote the Environmental Club at a football game. Hopefully it isn't one that will make me even more of a target for the team.

The varsity football coach's voice echoes in the gym as he praises the moral fiber of his players. The filled bleachers cheer his comments.

I think of Mr. Jackson and our meeting on Monday. "This isn't something that will get me in trouble, is it?"

Halle frowns. "That depends on what you mean by 'trouble.'"

"Trouble, as in the definition that my dean already hates me and another infraction could get me suspended."

She squeezes my arm. "Don't worry. I wouldn't do that to you, Baxter."

God help me, I believe her. So I relax and enjoy her company. I even clap a few times, caught up in the spirit of the mob mentality. I'm eager to go to the game, to see Halle away from school, to be with her for a few more hours. I haven't yet asked Mom if I can go. But a football game is a teenage ritual, and Mom wants me to fit in. How can she possibly say no?

A Note from My Past

The yellow manila envelope is perched against the screen door, but I don't notice it right away. It's only when I'm closing the door behind me that it falls down and I see it. The first thing that strikes me is that it's addressed to me. It can't be from the Mesothelioma Research Association already. Besides, Eddie's the contact person for that.

The return address is in California. Maybe it's from Dr. Anderson or Coyote. I look at the scrawled letters on the front and feel the blood drain from my face. It's Dink's handwriting. *How?*

In the two seconds it takes me to slam the door and secure the lock I'm sure he'll grab me from behind, but he doesn't. I drop to the floor and push the envelope away from me as though it's full of toxic dust that's set to explode or kill me with fumes when I open it. The idea doesn't seem all that implausible. I'm out of window range, but the phone is on the opposite counter. Should I call the police? I've got to tell someone.

I do a belly squirm across the floor and pick up the phone, but my hand stops on the buttons. The fact that he sent an envelope from California doesn't mean he's here in Minnesota. He'd have to break parole to travel here. Would that be enough to scare him away?

The envelope. It's waiting for me. I reach down with trembling hands and open it and peer inside. A single piece of paper. I remove it and read the numbers printed on it, the numbers I wrote down for Dink three years ago. This piece of paper hadn't made it into Dink's desk. I wonder where he kept it all this time. I can still recite the numbers in my head.

The paper is a message from Dink to me. He knows where I live. He's coming to get me.

I spend the next two hours on the floor waiting for Mom to come home. By the time she's due, though, I've had time to think. And one thing I think about is the fact that if Dink wanted to get me, he could have waited at the back door and grabbed me when I came home.

But he didn't. He's trying to scare me, like the time when he showed me his gargoyle tattoo and I spent hours hiding under my bed. He's playing mind games. He wants me to get so scared that I'll hand over the money the second I see him. But I don't have the money anymore, and I wouldn't give it to him anyway.

So I drag myself up off the floor and call Brad because I'm supposed to work tomorrow. I make up an excuse for why I can't come. I'm not sure Dink would approach me at the farm, and with Brad there beside me, I'd feel kind of safe. But what if Dink is carrying a gun or some other kind of weapon? I don't want Brad or his family to get hurt.

Then there's the football game tomorrow night. I can't even think of canceling that. Halle would hate me if I did. But how can I go if there's even a remote possibility that Dink is in town? If I tell Mom about the envelope, will she even let me go?

I slump back down on the floor. I'm trapped in my own house.

Forgetting

Mom has to work on Saturday. I lock the door the instant she leaves and I don't open the curtains. But the phone doesn't ring all day, and I'm too scared to check the mail. I peek out the door once and I don't see any sign of Dink or envelopes stuck in the door.

I didn't say anything to Mom. Despite my fear, I have to go to that game, and if I tell her that Dink knows where we live, she might not let me go. I'll tell her tonight after the football game. Then we can deal with it. Besides, I'm beginning to think that I overreacted. I mean, if Dink actually showed up at our house and we called the police, he'd go back to prison. Maybe Dink is still in California, trying to think of ways to get at me from there.

By the time Mom comes home, I've convinced myself that I'll be safe at the game tonight. I'll be surrounded by hundreds of other people and security guards. Dink wouldn't approach me there.

At 5:47 Mom brings home takeout, but not from the Tin Cup. She picked up fried rice and lo mein from the restaurant down the street. I'm too nervous to eat, but not just because of Dink. I'm seeing Halle tonight and pulling a school prank. I have money for nachos and Cokes during halftime, in memory of our first unofficial date. But what if I get too hungry before halftime? I can't leave anything to chance tonight, so I eat some of the fried rice straight from the box.

Mom splits open a fortune cookie and eats half before she reads her fortune. "You will find romance in an unexpected place."

She smiles and pops the rest of the cookie in her mouth, then sticks the white paper fortune into her pocket. She believes in that kind of stuff. That a printed saying stuck in a cookie can bring her good luck in relationships. I want to ask if she read one like that the day she met Dink.

"I need a ride to school at seven-eighteen," I say. "I'm going to the football game." I figured out how long it would take to get there. I want to arrive ahead of Halle but not too early. That way I can stake out a place inside the fence where they take tickets and wait for her.

Mom's picking up a loose noodle from the edge of the box. "But I have a date with my boss tonight. Did you forget?" She stops mid-noodle, as soon as the words leave her mouth. She stares at me, open mouthed, her eyes wide as the realization hits her. I imagine that's how Daniel Tammet's mom might have felt if he'd missed his recitation of pi on the third decimal point. Daniel Tammet would have been even more shocked.

And that's pretty much how I feel. Baxter Green, the boy who remembers everything, forgot all about Mom's date. She told me on Monday at 5:53 p.m. But between filming Halle's speech and the visit to the tunnel and the editing work and Halle asking me to the football game and finding the envelope from Dink, I somehow . . . forgot. The word is like a razor in my throat. I actually forgot.

It feels weird, like I messed up big time, like something is terribly wrong. I set down the box of fried rice, feeling suddenly nauseous.

"What's wrong with me, Mom?"

Mom reaches over and feels my head, then she recovers and scrapes the noodle back into the box. "Nothing's wrong. You're just so involved in your new life that you're experiencing what everyone else does on a daily basis. That's perfectly normal, Baxter."

I can feel the blood drain from my face. "Not for me, it isn't."

"You're reading too much into this. I'll see if Dan can drop you off on our way. I'm sure it's no bother. But how will you get home afterward?"

How will I get home? Have I forgotten that, too? "I can get a ride," I say with uncertainty. I'm not really sure who would take me.

"Good. I'll call Dan." She nudges me as she leaves the room. "Relax, Baxter. It's not that big a deal. Probably just stress."

Stress? Then why didn't I forget something years ago when Dink slapped me in his office, or when I had to testify in front of the judge and Dink was there? No, it's probably more than stress. Much more, like a tumor or cancer of the brain—or worse, white noise filling up my mind forever.

I fumble in my pocket and pull out Dr. Anderson's number. I don't trust myself to remember it right now. I don't trust myself to remember anything. I recite page 167 of *The Great Gatsby* in my head, then I recite page 8 of *The Weekly Reader*, the one I read six years ago. Okay, maybe I haven't completely lost it yet.

I wait until I hear Mom get off the phone and retreat to her room to get ready for her date before I dial his number. It's two hours earlier in California. Will Dr. Anderson still be in his office? He answers on the third ring. Just the sound of his voice helps me breathe.

"Dr. Anderson. This is Baxter. Baxter Green."

"Baxter. How nice to hear from you. How are things in Minnesota?"

"Not so good."

"Are you okay?"

"I forgot that my mom has a date, I mean an engagement." I'm still not admitting that Mom has a date. After all, she said he was just a friend. "She told me on Monday and I *forgot*."

"Oh." There's a pause on the phone. I imagine Dr. Anderson is thinking of a way to break the bad news that I'm doomed, that I'll soon be a ghost of the former Baxter who can't remember anything, as the tremendous amount of useless information fights for control with the important data until I no longer have any logical pattern of thought.

"Congratulations, Baxter."

"What?"

"That's good to hear. Remember when we talked about the filtering of memory, how most people focus their attention on those bits of information that they deem relevant?"

"Yes. So the irrelevant details don't become a distraction. But this was an important detail that I should have remembered."

"Perhaps. How do you feel about your mother's date?"

Like a thousand knots are squeezing down inside my stomach. "I don't know."

His voice grows soft. "Is it something you might not want to remember?"

I shake my head. "That's never been a factor before. I always remember everything."

"I know. You remember everything, even those details that are useless and can become detrimental. But you have to remember that the evolutionary purpose of memory is survival, to provide us with useful information and to avoid mistakes that we or others have made in the past. I'm wondering if forgetting this particular detail isn't perhaps a survival technique."

"You mean I wanted to forget it?"

"Exactly. Listen, Baxter. I don't know why you carry all this detailed information with you, why you don't forget things. It's a mystery. If I knew the answer, I'd have the Nobel Prize on my desk right now. But I do know that forgetting one detail isn't as tragic as it seems to you right now."

I press a hand to my forehead and close my eyes. "What if I keep forgetting?"

"Then you'll be like everyone else in the world. I wish I could tell you more, Baxter. We don't have the technology to image brain function with sufficient resolution. But we are doing more studies, and people like you help us understand more about human memory and brain function."

His voice is calm. I feel the stress drain away, like water rushing from a sink that's been plugged up too long. It's always nice to hear his voice. Reassuring in a way I can't put into words.

I almost don't want to hang up. I'd never have made it these past three years if Dr. Anderson hadn't been in my life. He was a researcher, but he'd been a therapist as well. How would he feel about my attempt to reinvent myself? Do I dare tell him what I'm doing?

"I'm back in school again." It's the most I feel comfortable saying.

"That's good news. How is it going?"

"Good." Well, except for the Dink part.

"You know, if you've been practicing trying to forget the trivial details like we worked on, that could be part of the reason you forgot your mom's event. Plus, you have the added pressure of school now."

"Maybe. Look, I have to leave for the football game in a few minutes. Dr. Anderson, can I call you again sometime?"

"Absolutely. I'd love to talk more. The phone number I gave you is my cell phone. Feel free to call at any time."

"I will. And thanks."

I hang up and sigh. Maybe he's right. Maybe it's not the beginning of the end. Maybe my brain won't disintegrate into white noise. Maybe I'll still remember my kindergarten teacher's name. Maybe.

How Fun Becomes
Part of My Vocabulary

"What do you think?" Mom puts her arms out. She's wearing a low-cut red dress that flares out at the bottom. I've never seen it before.

"Is that new?"

"I bought it yesterday. Wait, you have to get the full effect." She turns around and her dress twirls up.

"Cool," I say, thinking of her date and imagining a Minnesota version of Dink. He's laid off from the taconite plant, drives a pickup truck, drinks Grain Belt beer, and says "You bet" a lot.

Mom stops twirling and studies me. "I know you don't trust me."

"What do you mean?"

"I mean you weren't the only one who was in therapy these

last three years, Baxter. I know I made a huge mistake with Dink. I picked a guy who turned out to be a jerk. I exposed you to danger."

I don't say anything because it's true. Why rub her face in it?

Mom is wringing her hands. "I've had a hard time forgiving myself for everything Dink did to you and me and us as a family. I've had a hard time getting over him. He was kind of like a drug, I guess. And I'm still kicking the habit."

I think of Dink more as a disease than a drug.

Mom sighs. "I haven't had a date in three years. But I think it's time to start fresh. Both of us. Is that okay?"

I let out a breath. "So . . . this is a date now?"

Mom shrugs. "Sort of. We're taking it slow. I mean, he's my boss. We work together, so we're mostly just friends right now."

The doorbell rings.

"Are you sure you're okay with it?" Mom asks, even though she's walking toward the door as she asks. If I say no, will she cancel her date?

"I guess," I say without much conviction.

"You look great," a deep voice bellows through the open door.

"Dan, this is my son, Baxter."

Mom puts her arm around me as though I'm ten instead of fifteen, as though I'm not two inches taller than her.

Dan Peterson is a big, broad man with fat fingers that grasp my hand in a firm grip like I'm a piece of meat to be inspected. Not thin and wiry like Dink. I imagine him in the kitchen of the Tin Cup, his large form filling up the space between the fryers and grills as he cooks.

"You got a good grip, Baxter. Ever think of playing football?"

"Not really."

Mom puts her hands out. "See what I mean? New town, new opportunities."

Yeah, I'd fit right in with the football team.

"Your mom tells me you're good at remembering details."

I shoot her a look. Mom smiles in an awkward manner. Evidently I'm not the only one having trouble concealing things.

"If you ever need a job, let me know. We can always use a good worker."

"Thanks," I say.

"He's baling hay this fall," Mom says in a prideful voice. "He's strong *and* smart."

"Well, look me up when you're ready for a job in town."

"I will, Mr. Peterson."

I'm grateful that he doesn't say "call me Dan." It would have been so Dink-like.

I ride in the backseat of the Chrysler van, an older model that somehow makes me feel better about the whole night. I'm not sure how I feel about Dan Peterson, but at least he's not a flashy guy.

Mom and Mr. Peterson talk about work, about the new club in town, about the Lutheran Church, which Mom claims affiliation to but has never attended as far as I know. I watch for Dink's Camaro.

As we pull into the parking lot of the school, Mom asks about my ride home. "We can pick you up afterward," Mr. Peterson offers.

"That's okay. I'll catch a ride with friends." I say it so naturally that I believe it myself. I don't want to ride home with Mom's date. I'm sure Eddie will give me a ride.

"Will you be warm enough?" Mom asks.

I'm wearing my winter coat, which is too big for me, but which Mom is afraid I'll grow out of since I shot up so much over the summer.

"I'm fine. Thanks for the ride." I open the door and pause. "Mr. Peterson, have you ever been in a fight?"

He lets out a deep laugh. "Are you kidding? I grew up on the wrong side of Duluth. I learned to throw a punch. But I don't fight if I can avoid it."

He's twice the size of Dink. It makes me feel better knowing he can take care of Mom if Dink does ever show up.

"Why did you ask that?" Mom's voice is tense.

"Don't worry, Mom. I'm not doing any fighting tonight." I close the door and wave as they pull away. Mr. Peterson sounds like a marshmallow, a thought that consoles me as I turn to face the cold wind.

The stadium is already half-full, with orange-and-black colors on the right side and red on the left. The band is warming up, their instruments bellowing out spurts of cascading notes. The smell of popcorn and hot dogs drifts up from the concession stand. The lights of the stadium flood the night sky. Football is in the air.

Then I see Hunter and his friends near the bleachers. I move into the darkness, willing myself to become invisible.

"You're here!" Halle's exuberant voice floats out in a breath of white air. So much for beating her here. She gives me a quick hug, then pulls me behind the crowd. We stand alone in the dark, save for flashes of light that peek through openings in the bleachers. Her hair sticks out beneath a white knit cap and the cold air makes her eyelashes appear glittery.

She looks up at me and I'm overcome with that sensation again, the same one that makes me do irrational things before I can stop myself. But Halle reaches up and puts her lips on mine before I can even talk myself out of kissing her. Her soft lips send a wave of warmth through my whole body.

She pulls back and smiles. "This way you can concentrate on your task instead of thinking about kissing me all night."

I don't know where my confidence comes from, but I bend down and kiss her again. "As if this will keep me from thinking about it?"

She smiles and shakes her head. "I'm getting a huge crush on you, Baxter."

I want to tell her that I have the same crush on her, that it's karma or fate or whatever you want to call it. That we were meant to be together, that our moving here had as much to do with destiny as with my movement of the map. But that sounds cliché, and the moment passes too quickly. She opens her backpack and takes out a piece of paper.

"The halftime show tonight is a tribute to our dear old Wellington Mines. The band members are changing into flannel shirts and miner hats and playing the song 'Coal Miner's Daughter' and ending with 'We Will Rock You.' Between songs we thought it would be nice to make a tribute of our own. So we've written down the names of as many people as we could come up with who have died from mesothelioma."

She hands me the sheet. There's a list of eighteen names, with dates next to them. "What am I supposed to do with this?"

Halle lets out a short breath. "I have a friend in the announcer's booth. You'll have thirty seconds of airtime between songs while the band moves into position."

"You want me to read these names?"

"The names and the dates of death."

"He's okay with that?"

"Well, Ace doesn't exactly know that's what you're reading."

"And how is this *not* going to get me expelled?"

"For what? For a tiny halftime prank? It's pretty harmless. They can't expel you for that. Besides, you're hidden from view up there. And Ace is a good guy. He won't narc on you afterward."

Halle takes my hand. "You're the only one in our club who doesn't have someone working at the plant. Besides, it will be fun. And you'll be making a statement."

Fun hasn't been in my vocabulary for a long time, if ever. And I can still taste Halle on my lips, making it difficult to think. But I know that no matter what she says, I could get in trouble. If not from the administration, then from the band and football team. Should I take such a risk just to impress her?

I fold the sheet of paper in half and stick it in my pocket. I smile at Halle, the smile of a guy drunk, not on alcohol, but on daffodils, thousands and thousands of them. She's the only reason that I smile every day. Hell yes, I'll do it.

The Problem of the List

The Mental Club has staked out a spot near the top of the bleachers. Blankets and seat cushions, a tub of buttered popcorn, and a thermos of hot chocolate are waiting for us. A hero's welcome, Halle says, and it makes sense because I feel as though I'm being sent into battle.

"My man," Eddie says, bumping fists. "I've been working on another video, this one for the choir. I could use some help."

"Sure. I'll go in early next week if you give me a ride."

"It's a deal."

The football team bursts onto the field amid cheers while the marching band plays the school song. Students clap their mittens and gloves together in muted applause.

Halle sits next to me, our legs touching. Her breath spreads up onto my neck as she huddles closer, trying to keep warm. Who'd have guessed that cold was so sexy?

"You've been working out," she teases as she squeezes my upper arm.

"I owe it all to Brad and about eight hundred hay bales."

Last night I thought my life was over. And tonight I'm sitting next to the girl of my dreams and she's looking at me like I'm her Prince Charming, the man she's waited for her entire life. Funny how fast things can change.

But beneath my happiness a feeling of dread gnaws at my insides. I've spent the last two months trying to blend in and be unrecognizable. A blur among the student population of Madison High. And it hasn't been easy. Now I'm about to do something that will make me stand out above the crowd and draw attention. My instincts fight against it.

I try to enjoy the game. The Madison High Tigers are getting clobbered. The other team runs through them like they're dominoes instead of one-hundred-eighty-pound linebackers. The guy who sounds like twice-baked potatoes fumbles the ball on the twenty yard line, giving the other team an easy shot at a touchdown.

We're in the second quarter, with two minutes left, when Halle tells me it's time to go. She leads me up the stairs to the announcer's booth. The marching band is already assembled on the track, ready to take the field.

"Just knock when halftime is here," she says. "Ace knows you're coming. And don't be nervous. Do you have the list?"

I pull it out of my pocket.

Halle frowns. "Let me see it a moment." She unfolds the paper and reads down. Her hands start to shake. "I wrote the date of his funeral instead of his death. How could I have done that?"

Her voice cracks and is replaced by a frantic tone. "Do you have a pencil or something to write with?"

"No. Sorry."

"God, I'm such an idiot."

I put my hands on her shoulders. "It's okay. Tell me the date. I can remember it."

Her eyes are wet. "January 23, 2009. That's what it should read next to Henry Calvin Phillips."

"January 23, 2009. Got it," I say, and I flash a convincing smile.

She sniffs and gives me a hug. "Thank you, Baxter. You don't know what this means to me, to all of us. This prank is going to make you immortal. We'll be waiting behind the bleachers afterward. Eddie's taking us all out for victory pizza."

She leaves at 8:30, just as the buzzer signals halftime. The Tigers are down seventeen to three and they look downcast as they walk off the field. If it weren't for pizza, I'd enjoy staying for the second half to see them get beat even worse.

The band marches out onto the field and gets into position. The lights go out and the crowd responds with "oohs" and "ahhs" and a few shrieks. Then the announcer's voice booms out from the speaker above my head.

"Ladies and gentlemen, tonight we present a special tribute to our town's heritage, the Wellington Miners. Please give a round of applause to the Madison High marching band."

Each band member wears a helmet with a light above it, and now those lights come on, all one hundred eighty-six of them, and the band starts playing. They look like a field of marching fireflies as they move in unison.

I feel like I have as many fireflies in my stomach as I look at the list. I'm supposed to knock on the door, but I can't quite bring myself to do it. I put my hand out and stop. God, I'm such a wimp, a total failure. I don't want to be immortal. Why can't Halle understand that? I want to be like everyone else.

I'm a coward. I just can't do this. I start walking away when I bump into someone, causing me to drop the list.

"Mr. Green," a familiar voice makes me catch my breath. Mr. Jackson waves a small flashlight in front of me.

"What have you got there?" he asks, picking up the paper before I have a chance to grab it.

"Nothing."

He focuses the flashlight's beam on the list.

"It's for our club. The Environmental Club. It's personal," I protest, but Mr. Jackson is already reading it out loud. "The following people have died from mesothelioma, a cancer caused by working in Wellington's mines? This isn't true."

"We think it is."

"Just what are you planning to do with this?" He looks at the announcer's booth and his mouth falls open.

Even though I wimped out, no way am I confessing my plans to Mr. Jackson. I shrug. "Nothing."

"Nothing is right. I don't want to see this anarchist type of material on our campus ever again. Do you understand?"

I let out a laugh. "Anarchist? Just because Wellington Mines owns the whole town?"

Mr. Jackson folds up the sheet of paper until it's the size of a coaster. "This is what I think of your list." He tears it in two, then tears those pieces in two.

The blood rises up inside me, letting loose an anger I haven't felt in years. "You have no right to do that," I spit out.

Mr. Jackson nods. "Sorry, I just did." He throws the pieces up into the wind, scattering them in the darkness. "Have a nice evening, Mr. Green."

He leaves me in the darkness as the band plays the final segments of "Coal Miner's Daughter." I'm supposed to be inside preparing to read the list.

I don't know what to do. Mr. Jackson can't do this to me, to our club. It's not fair, and I know all about being treated unfairly. Dink used me because I was a kid who didn't know any better. I may be a wimp, but I'm not going to let Mr. Jackson get away with this.

I don't bother to knock.

"Halle sent me," I say to the guy in the booth, who looks to be in his mid-twenties. Ace is sitting in the cramped booth reading a Stephen King novel beneath a pea-sized light on the desk. "I'm making an announcement."

Ace jumps. "I thought you were a zombie." Then he laughs. "Just a sec." He stands and has me sit in front of the microphone. "Flip this switch when you're ready. The band is almost done playing the song. They'll be moving into position for the next one. That's when you can talk, but you'll only have about thirty seconds, so make it quick."

"Okay." I try to steady my voice. I think of Mr. Jackson and the pieces of the list carried away by the wind, and the constant threat of Dink. The anger pushes me forward. The band finishes and the crowd applauds. I turn on the microphone and speak in a clear, deep voice.

"My fellow students, the Environmental Club wants to give tribute to those people who spent their lives working at Wellington Mines. The following is a list of people who died from mesothelioma, a cancer thought to be caused from exposure to taconite dust."

I say each name and date, all eighteen of them. I'd locked the door when I entered in case Mr. Jackson tried to stop me. And then there's Ace. When I look over at him, he's clapping silently and nodding. After I announce all eighteen names I say, "Let's give them the recognition they deserve." The crowd cheers until the band breaks into, "We Will Rock You."

"Good going," Ace says, and shakes my hand. "You can go out this door if you want." He motions to a door on the other side of the booth. "It's closer."

"Thanks." I wonder if Ace knows that Mr. Jackson is waiting outside the other door.

I hurry out into the darkness and run down the darkened steps, almost tripping on the way down. I did it! And I feel so alive in doing it, so satisfied. As though I just jammed a fist in Mr. Jackson's paunch, or stuck a knife in Dink's gargoyle tattoo. It feels that good.

I dash behind the bleachers, searching for my friends.

"Baxter!" Eddie high-fives me in a sliver of light. "Unbelievable! You did it!"

Gina hugs me. "That was pure magic! Your voice in the darkness, reading the names of those miners while a field of band students marched around with miner hats, their little lights glowing."

Roxie kisses my cheek. "I bawled the whole time. It was so awesome."

"It felt good," I say. "Where's Halle? It was her idea, you know." Then I see her. She's not smiling, not jumping up and down like everyone else. She's standing in the darkness, and it's only when I'm right in front of her that I see the odd expression on her face.

"How?" she asks. "How did you do it? You only looked at the list once, for just a second."

"What do you mean . . . ?"

"I came back up when I saw Mr. Jackson shred the paper and throw it away," she says, with more force in her voice. "So how did you memorize all those names? You even got my grandpa's death correct. How did you do it?"

"What does it matter? He did it!" Gina says behind me. "He was amazing."

I stare at Halle. I want to explain what she's already figuring out on her own. I can see it in her expression. The expression that says she sees me differently now.

She looks at me, challenging me to deny it. Her eyes are slits. "Baxter. That strange boy who memorized movies. That was his name."

My throat goes tight.

"It's you, isn't it?"

I stare at her. What can I say? "Surprise?"

She turns away.

"I meant to tell you," I say.

She spins toward me. "You knew all this time?"

"What are you talking about?" Gina asks. "What boy?"

I look at Gina. What lie do I have up my sleeve this time? I've got nothing. "We knew each other."

"When?"

"Years ago, back in kindergarten. Halle didn't remember me until now."

Gina shrugs. "So you knew each other in kindergarden. Why is that a big deal?"

"It's not like I lied to you," I say, turning back around, but it's too late. Halle has disappeared into the darkness.

Facing My Demons

I end up walking home. As much as I'm scared shitless about seeing Dink on the way, I'm just as scared that Hunter will catch up with me or I'll freeze to death before I make it home. I should have asked Eddie for a ride. But I ran after Halle, who disappeared into the crowd, and by the time I returned Eddie and the rest of them had left. Then Hunter saw me and I ran.

I cram my hands into my coat pockets to keep the biting cold from causing frostbite, and drape my hood over my head, but my ears sting and my nose is running and my cheeks feel tight. By the time I reach our street, my legs are stiff. Even my eye sockets hurt.

I've been thinking about it the whole way home; how my best day became my worst, how the whole night was doomed from the start. If I'd stayed home because of Dink or had wimped out and not announced the names, Halle might have dumped me, but when I did announce the names she dumped me anyway. Why did I think I could pull it off?

I'd hoped that by the time Halle found out who I really was, it wouldn't matter anymore. I was wrong. Of course it mattered. Halle ended up being just as superficial as Daisy in *Gatsby*. How ironic. I'd convinced myself it was just a book, that it didn't have any connection to real life.

I'm rounding the corner when I see a car outside our house. Is Mom home already? I pull up my coat sleeve and check my watch. It's 10:11. Still early.

I stop twenty feet away. My heart beats fast. A figure leans against the car, only the lighted end of a cigarette visible.

The man sees me. He throws his cigarette into the grass and walks toward me.

Gargoyle tattoo.

Stilted laugh.

Wild, marble eyes.

Hot flashes of anger.

Muddy water.

I'm ten years old again, hiding under my bed as hands reach in to grab me, and the walls are collapsing all around. I'm losing it. I close my eyes and fight for control. Make this whole day a bad dream. Make it go away.

I open my eyes and Dink is in front of me, the same wiry frame and familiar stance. He's wearing a wrinkled suit, as though he slept in it. "Is that you, Baxter? Why, you've grown a whole lot since I last saw you."

A shiver works its way up my already-frozen spine. I try to keep my voice even. "We don't want to see you."

"My God, even your voice has changed. You're all grown up now, aren't you?"

"We don't want to see you," I repeat.

"But I want to see you. Don't you remember all those good times we had together?"

"I remember everything," I say through gritted teeth.

"That's right. You have that amazing memory thing going on. Too bad you're wasting it. I could have made you rich, you know, if you hadn't gone off and turned me in like a lame ass-hole. But you got some of my money anyway, didn't you?"

I don't answer. There's no use denying what Dink already knows.

Dink looks toward the house. "Is your mom home? I've missed her something awful these past three years."

"No! Leave now before I call—"

Dink takes a step closer, close enough that I smell alcohol on his dank breath. He slurs slightly when he speaks. "Call who? The police? Are you going to confess to stealing my money? I know you took it, you little bastard, and I'm not leaving until I get it. One way or another."

I stand head-to-head with Dink, and I realize that he's right. I'm three years older and as tall as him. I've built muscle hauling fifty-pound bales of hay. I've wrestled with Brad and his brother. And I'm not about to give Dink the money.

"It's gone."

"Gone where?"

"I spent it. There's nothing left."

"You spent my money?"

"You lived in our house, Mom's house, for eleven months

and you only helped with the rent twice, on January 6 and October 10. I heard Mom ask you to pay and you always had some excuse, like you were behind on alimony payments to your ex-wife, and you always promised her that you'd make it up to her later but you never did. And now it's gone. So, yeah, I spent *our* money."

"I don't believe you. What did you spend sixty-five thousand dollars on?"

"Sixty-five thousand, three hundred fifty-eight dollars and ninety-seven cents. I gave it to charity."

He shakes his head. "No. You're lying. Nobody gives sixty-five thousand dollars to charity. Not even a freak like you."

I take a step closer. I'm face-to-face with Dink, the man I've spent all this time thinking about, who kept me awake at night, who I feared I'd see every time I turned a corner. And now he's really here. But I'm not that kid anymore. "You're not getting your money back."

The fist comes from Dink's right and connects with my left jaw. I stumble back, stunned by the strength of the hit. Tears spring into my eyes and I push them back down.

I put my hand on my throbbing jaw. I've never fought anyone in my life, but my fingers curve into fists, the anger working its way down into them. I throw a punch at Dink's face and somehow make contact. He falls backward and clutches his nose. Bright red blood flows out. It almost makes me puke. I think I broke it.

Dink seems surprised that I hit him. He steps back and wipes his nose on his sleeve. Then his face hardens. "I've been in prison for three years. You think I can't take a kid like you?"

"It doesn't matter. You're leaving."

He walks around me, his feet moving back and forth like a drunken prize fighter. "Okay, let's see what you got, Baxter."

I barely register the headlights of an oncoming car. We're in the middle of the street in the freezing air, but my focus is on Dink. The Boogeyman might be a pathetic loser, but he throws a hard punch and I don't want to take my eyes off him.

I hear tires squealing and Mom's voice. "Baxter!" I look away and Dink hits me before I can get my arms up to block it. He flattens me with a punch to the side of the head. I hit the ground hard. My head is spinning and I don't think I can get up.

"You ready to give me my money now?"

I cough out bits of gravel. "I told you. I don't have it."

Dink grabs me by the shirt and pulls me up on my knees. His eyes are wild and angry. "Then you better find it!"

"Not going to happen," I say in a ragged breath. I mentally prepare myself for the next hit, which may kill me. At least I won't have to remember this moment when I'm dead. My past flashes through my mind; random moments: my dad reading me a story book, Halle chasing me in a game of tag on the playground, the first sentence from Gatsby, Dr. Anderson's phone number.

I've zoned out, which is probably a good thing. But my mind flashes to the image of Gatsby floating facedown in his swimming pool, and I decide I shouldn't go down without more of a fight. So I take a swing at Dink. I'm not sure if I connect or not, but I hear a loud crack and Dink lets go. He crumples next to me on the street.

Mom is standing above him with the rake in her hand.

"Oh my God! What did he do to you, Baxter?"

She brings the rake above her head to hit Dink again but Dan stops her. "I don't think he's getting back up, Mary."

Dan has already called the police. He reaches down. "Are you all right, Baxter?"

"I'm alive!" I'm so hyped that I ignore the pain in my knuckles and the throbbing of my head. I hardly notice Mom's frantic cries. Dan pulls me up to a sitting position. I look down at Dink and smile. I let Mom put a tissue over my bleeding nose and I bend over, still elated, as though I was the one who knocked Dink out. It's like I just overdosed on caffeine, the same way I felt after making that announcement earlier.

It isn't until the red lights of the police cars light up the neighborhood and the whole street fills with people that I start to breathe normally again. There's a blanket draped across my shoulders, but I don't know how it got there.

"He could have killed you." Mom is crying, and Dan puts an arm around her.

"But he didn't. I stood up to him. And so did you, Mom."

Dan whistles. "I think you broke his nose, Baxter."

"I hope so."

"And he's going to have quite a headache, Mary."

Mom just looks down at Dink and shakes her head.

He finally comes to, but an ambulance has been called and he acts dazed and puts his hand over his nose and head.

We go inside where it's warm and the police talk with Mom and Dan.

They ask me some questions and I answer them all

honestly, with the exception of the money. I only say that Dink wanted revenge because I testified against him.

"He broke his parole and assaulted a kid," the officer says. "You won't be hearing from him anytime soon."

It's not until after the police leave and Mom makes hot chocolate and I'm sitting at the kitchen table with the warm cup in my shaking hands that it hits me. I'm not scared of him anymore. I've stared death in the face, taken my licks, and still lived to talk about it.

Mom shakes her head. "I hate to think of what would have happened if we hadn't come home then." She puts her finger on my bruised jaw. "I'm so sorry, Baxter. This is all my fault."

"It's okay, Mom."

"Do you want to move again?" she asks. "I'll do anything you want."

I shake my head. "And let Dink control our lives? I'm not afraid of him anymore. Let's let Dink do the running from now on."

She sighs. "Oh God. What must the neighbors think of us now?"

I remember what Eddie said about the Iron Range. "That we're blue-collar, beer-drinking, hell-raising miners?"

Dan laughs. "Then I guess you're in the right place."

The Rules and Regulations of Madison High School

First thing Monday morning I stop at Halle's locker, but she's nowhere to be found. I head for class, but Mr. Jackson summons me to his office before the first bell rings. He walks back and forth in front of me, his arms crossed as though he watches a lot of detective shows and knows the ins and outs of interrogation. He stops and pulls up the sleeves of his sweater.

"What happened to your face? Are you all right?"

I touch my tender jaw. My eye is black and blue, too. "I'm fine. I ran into a door."

"Or maybe you ran into something when you were hurrying out of the announcer's box in the dark?"

"No. That didn't happen." Not a lie.

He makes a *tsk* sound. "It seems the broadcaster suffered memory loss. He said he didn't know who made that announcement. And no one witnessed you do it. But I saw the list."

"You destroyed the list," I remind him.

"And you could have had a copy."

"I didn't."

Mr. Jackson doesn't have any real evidence, just circumstantial. I have a feeling that's not going to keep me out of detention.

"This is your second infraction within a month, Mr. Green. I don't think you realize how deep a hole you're digging for yourself."

"What rule did I break?"

"Well, first you didn't ask for permission to make an announcement."

"Would you have given me permission if I'd asked?"

"Of course not."

"But that's not a specific rule in the handbook."

He picks up the thick booklet. "So you did read it. Then you should know that the code of student conduct specifies that you are to respect and maintain school property."

"If I *was* the one who made the announcement, and I'm not saying I was, how would that have undermined respect for school property?"

"Any act disruptive to the educational process, including disobedience and disrespect."

"The information read was educational, not disruptive."

"Unauthorized usage."

"The announcer allowed it."

"But *I* didn't."

I don't respond. Let Mr. Jackson prove it was me.

"I recognized your voice."

"It could have been anyone." If he didn't actually see me do it, how could he be sure? I stare at the walls, at the diplomas and certificates of exemplary service. I study the floor and Mr. Jackson's brown loafers that are scuffed on the toes. When it becomes apparent that I'm not going to collapse and confess, Mr. Jackson lets out a long sigh. "Are you refusing to accept responsibility for your actions?"

I shrink back in my chair, but I shake my head defiantly.

Mr. Jackson's eyes narrow and the muscles in his neck tighten. He picks up the thick pamphlet of school rules. "Since you're attempting to quote the rules to me, then let's see how prepared you really are."

Maybe it's because I stood up to Dink Saturday night that I'm not shivering with fright. Or maybe because I read the rules. I nod at Mr. Jackson and feel my mouth curl up. "You're on."

What Does a Superhero Sound Like?

Halle's not in school. I wait by her locker until the period ends. Then I see Gina.

"She left the game without saying good-bye, hasn't answered my e-mails or phone calls, and now she's skipped," Gina says, shaking her head. "I'm so mad at her. We want to celebrate and she's being her moody self. Do you know what's got into her?"

"Um, I think she's mad at me."

"That's crazy. You were great! You're a freakin' hero!"

I shrug and go to class. Even though I never admitted my guilt, the rest of the school soon knows that I was being interrogated by Mr. Jackson. Combined with my swollen eye and reddened jaw, the rumors spread fast. Students high-five me in the hallway and say hi to me. They suddenly know my name.

"Best prank ever," says Jay, the ninth-grade student council rep.

"You're the man!" Brad slaps me on the back like I'm one of his heifers and I almost fall over. "And Jackson is an A-hole."

The football team heard about the halftime announcement, and instead of being angry, they think it's cool. They no longer act like they want to kill me. Even Hunter stays away. Maybe he feels sorry for me because I'm already bruised.

Only the band director and Mr. Jackson are upset. But I have to give Mr. Jackson credit. He's one of those strictly by-the-rules types, and he didn't have any evidence that I'd broken any. After I answered ten questions correctly, he let me go. He wasn't happy about it, though.

The irony grates on me. All I ever wanted was to be invisible, just another student in the crowd. Except with Halle. And now that I've done everything Halle asked of me, I am invisible to her. But not to everyone else.

The Environmental Club meets after school to celebrate. I wait outside the door, wondering if Halle will show up, wondering if I dare go in.

Eddie walks up behind me. "What are you doing in the hallway? Aren't you coming to the meeting?"

I study the closed door. "I'm not sure I'm wanted there."

"Are you kidding? You're the school hero."

I shake my head. "Not to everyone."

"I'm not sure what's going on between you and Halle, but I've known her a lot of years. She's a spitfire, but she'll settle down after a while."

"Does that mean I should stay out here?"

"Come on," he says, pulling me inside. "I have an announcement you need to hear."

There are four new girls at the meeting, but no Halle. They're talking to Gina and Roxie.

"Oh, this is him." Gina pulls me into the circle. "They're here because of you, Baxter."

"Me?"

"Yeah. Your announcement at the game last week. They want to join our club."

I recognize one of the girls from my lunch period. She sits at the performing arts table and eats plain vanilla yogurt every day.

"Those names you read," the girl says. "One of them was my uncle."

"Oh, I'm sorry."

"Don't be. I'm glad you did it. Nobody talks about him. Nobody admits what the taconite dust did to his lungs."

Roxie tells them about the video and shows them the case histories.

"Speaking of the video," Eddie says, "guess who got a letter this morning from the Mesothelioma Research Association?"

"Already?" Roxie looks crestfallen. "That didn't take long."

"Is it good news or bad news?" Gina asked.

Roxie puts her hands together in a prayer. "Don't read it if it's bad news."

Eddie hushes them. "I'm not reading anything until you're all quiet."

"Spill it," Gina says. "The suspense is killing me."

He puts a hand in the air. "First, the bad news: we didn't win the competition."

"I knew it," Gina says. "I never win anything."

"Hold on. Now the good news: they're working with the Department of Health, who will be starting an investigation into the link between taconite and mesothelioma."

All the girls shriek. Gina grabs Eddie and kisses him. Roxie jumps up and down. Then she hugs me and jumps up and down again.

"I wish Halle was here. Let's call her," Roxie says.

Gina frowns. "She's not answering her phone."

Eddie tips his head. "This is one meeting she's going to be sorry she missed."

"Read the whole letter. I want to hear every glorious word," Roxie says.

Eddie glances over at me before he opens up the paper and reads. "We are happy to announce that the Department of Health will complete a report on the elevated rate of mesothelioma in Northern Minnesota and its relation, if any, to the taconite industry. Furthermore, your support and commitment to preserving the quality of life in your town is exemplary, and in that regard, we've decided to honor your club with special recognition at our annual meeting on January 23, when we will show your video to the attendees and present you with a special certificate."

"That gives me the shivers," Roxie says. "It's like fate or something."

"Read it again," Gina says dreamily.

Eddie shakes his head and folds the paper. "Time to talk strategy. We want to get this news out in the community so more people will come forward. We need publicity. We need brainstorming. Girls?"

"I am so ready," Gina says. "I'm thinking book deal and movie rights. I'm going to make our club famous."

Roxie scratches her head. "You know, you just might."

The new girls join in the discussion. Eddie pulls me aside. "We need to talk. Outside."

I follow him into the hallway, where he opens the letter and squints at me. "I didn't read the whole letter out loud."

I nod. "I thought you might not have."

Eddie takes a breath and reads. "Your generous contribution definitely helped to make this happen. Even though you've asked to keep it private, we feel that your club deserves recognition for your commitment to preserving the quality of life in your town. Of course, we will continue to keep your financial support a secret."

He stops reading and looks up. "It says we contributed sixty-five thousand, three hundred fifty-eight dollars and ninety-seven cents. I almost passed out when I read that!"

I think of Halle, of how I'd wanted her to know about it when I sent it, of how happy I thought she'd be when she found out.

Eddie narrows his eyes. "I know Halle's dad didn't give us the money, and nobody else has any. You mailed the video, Baxter."

"Yes. I know."

"So?"

"Let's just say it was Dink's unintentional donation to our club."

"That's one hell of a donation. Did he have something to do with your face?"

"Yeah."

"Okay, I'm not going to ask a lot of questions. I'm not going to ask how you were able to memorize all those names or what went down with Dink or why you donated sixty-five thousand dollars instead of depositing it into the Baxter Green college fund."

"Good. And don't tell Halle about the money."

Eddie waves the paper in front of me. "Are you crazy? Halle would forgive you in an instant if she knew you did this. That money was the main reason they decided to do the study."

"I know. And I know it sounds nuts, but I don't want this to be the reason she forgives me."

"If I'd done something like this, I'd want everyone in the world to know about it. Man, I'm using that video for a class project, and I'm thinking of using it to get into the Graphic Design Program. You don't mind, do you, even though we worked on it together?"

"No. Not at all."

He puts the letter back into the envelope. "I just don't see what use it is to be the superhero if no one knows about it, especially the girl you want to impress. I mean, isn't that the whole point?"

"I want her to like me for who I am."

He raises his eyebrows. "What if you're a superhero?"

And suddenly, it makes me think. Maybe Eddie is right.

How Pi Contains the Answer to My Universe

Mr. Feege is one of those math geeks who really loves what he teaches. I don't share his enthusiasm for math, but I have to respect his determination to cram that love down our throats. He stands before the board, on which he's drawn the symbol for pi. "People have been using a value for pi since the Old Testament. Some people believe that pi contains the answer to the universe." He pauses to let it sink in, as though this enlightenment will somehow change our view of the assignment, over which most students are still whining. "So as we begin our competition today, let's think about how pi is like a never-ending circle, and how no pattern ever appears twice in the number, and it goes on forever. Who wants to go first?"

Everyone has to take a turn, whether they make it through ten digits or a hundred. I sink down in my desk. I have no intention of going first. I haven't even looked at the paper.

Jeb Danner jumps up, cocky and confident. He'll be lucky to make it through ten digits, but I doubt that Jeb cares, anyway.

Mr. Feege takes out a sheet of paper to keep the stats. "Start whenever you're ready, Jeb."

Jeb clears his throat and smiles. "3.14159265." He pauses.

Eight digits. I was right.

"35897 . . ." He pauses again, this time longer, his brows furrowed.

"Hey, that's my bank account number," Corey says from the back row, and even I laugh at that one.

Jeb scowls. "You broke my concentration. I have to repeat the last few numbers. Let's see, 6535897 . . ."

It isn't until I hear Jeb say it a second time that it strikes me. Sixty-five thousand, three hundred fifty-eight dollars and ninety-seven cents. My heart flops. It's right there in the digits of pi, a pattern that never repeats itself. What are the odds? Those numbers have been my whole universe for the past three years.

My God, Mr. Feege is right! Pi is the answer to *my* universe.

Jeb is still talking but I no longer hear him. There are coincidences in life, and there are forces that point you in a new direction, a tiny spot on the map where you can be someone different. But maybe that new person will cause you to lose your real self. I'm so tired of hiding and pretending. I'm so tired of trying to fit in when clearly I don't.

I tried to change who I am, like Jay Gatsby, who was ashamed of his past and never thought he was good enough for Daisy, and maybe that's why he lost her. Maybe I lost Halle because of who I pretended to be instead of who I really am. I never gave her a chance to like the real Baxter, perfect memory, strange quirks, and all. Like Eddie said, what's the point in being a superhero if nobody knows about it?

I pick up the sheet that Mr. Feege handed out, the one that lists a thousand digits of pi. I didn't ask for this memory, but like the digits of pi, it's a mystery that's waiting to be solved. I look at the sheet and raise my hand, fully aware that math class will never be the same again.

The Daffodil Dance

Two hours later I find Eddie. "Halle's absent again. Can you give me a ride to her house?"

"Gina called her. She's not home. And now she's in big trouble. Her mom and dad know that she skipped school today. What happened between you two?"

I sigh. "She hates me. She thinks I'm a freak."

"Does it have something to do with you reciting one thousand digits of pi in math class?"

"You heard about that already?"

"News travels fast. Everyone's talking about it. First the prank and now this. You're making quite a name for yourself."

I let out a breath. "I didn't mean to."

"So, what's with the memory thing?"

I steel myself for his reaction. "I have a photographic memory and I don't forget anything."

Eddie's eyebrows go up. "You mean you *never* forget? Like an elephant?"

"I never thought of myself as an elephant before, but yeah, I guess we do have that in common. That and tusks."

He laughs. "That's pretty impressive. You made Mr. Feege's year. He's already talking about entering you into a national contest. So, that's how you were able to recite all those names and dates at the football game. You really *are* a superhero."

"Not according to Halle."

He flashes me one of his knowing looks. "Well, maybe you're a mutant. Or maybe you need to use your superpowers to convince her."

"I don't even know where she is."

"She's probably hiding out."

"Hiding out? Where?"

Eddie flicks my forehead with his finger. "You know, for someone with a great memory, you suck at figuring out clues."

Sometimes I am *so* slow. "Oh, right."

"I'll give you a ride, but you'll have to find it on your own from the road. Is your memory really that good?"

"Not a problem."

Thirty minutes later Eddie drops me off on a gravel road at the edge of the forest. "You want to borrow my cell phone in case you get lost?"

"I won't get lost," I assure him. "I remember the way there."

He tosses it to me anyway. "In case she's not there and you need a ride back."

"Thanks."

He nods. "I knew there was something about you. I mean, who remembers where the middle of the freakin' US is?"

I shrug. "An elephant or a mutant superhero."

"Why keep it a secret?"

"Why keep your cancer a secret?"

Eddie sighs. "I guess we both have our reasons."

"Well, I'm kind of glad my secret's out, regardless of the consequences."

He taps the wheel. "Something to keep in mind. Good luck with Halle. And just for the record, nobody should make you feel like a freak just because you're different."

I get out of the van with a new resolve. Eddie's right again. I'm the one who should be mad at Halle, not the other way around. But by the time I've made my way to the cave, the only thing I can think of is escaping the bitter cold.

There's a small light coming from the tunnel. I crawl through the hole and stand up when I get inside. A tall lantern is perched on a flat rock, spreading light out onto the rocky walls. Halle sits next to it on a blanket with her legs crossed. She looks up from the book she's reading as though she's not surprised to see me, as though she's been waiting for me all day.

She points to a spot next to her on the blanket. "Have a seat."

I sit next to her. Our legs touch and the indignant fire that was blazing in my stomach when I got out of the truck is little more than a piece of lukewarm charcoal now.

She hands me the book. A greenish tear falls from the sad eyes on the cover of *Gatsby*. Those eyes stare up at me and I'm overwhelmed with pity for the poor little rich girl.

Halle looks at me. "You didn't really need a tutor, did you?"

I shrug. "I guess not."

"Then why pretend?"

I can't help but look at the book's cover as I tell her the truth. "I had this stupid idea that I could be someone else. Someone completely different than the Memory Boy. Someone you'd like."

"I did like you," she says softly.

Great. She said "did," as in she no longer feels that way.

She picks up the book. "You and Gatsby have a lot in common."

"Gatsby was a much better liar than I am."

"He had more practice."

"I didn't mean to lie. Especially to you."

She sniffs. It's not enough. She hates me. Either that or she's catching a cold. "Did you get in trouble at school?" she asks.

"Not really. Everyone thought it was cool."

She reaches up. I flinch when her finger touches my jaw. "You should see the other guy," I say.

"My dad heard about the football game stunt."

"Did *you* get in trouble?" Maybe that's why she's hiding out in a freezing cave.

"He thought I had something to do with it, but he couldn't really accuse me. He said that whoever did it was misguided."

She shakes her head. "He grew up here. He said he'd never put the lives of family and friends at risk. I think he really meant it. He said that if he thought the taconite dust really caused all those deaths, he'd start a study himself."

"He doesn't have to. Eddie got a letter from the Mesothelioma Research Association. The Department of Health is beginning a study on the elevated rates of mesothelioma and the taconite plants and mines."

She gasps. "Really? Are you kidding me?"

"Really." I still can't mention the donation, even if it means she'll forgive me, seeing as how it wasn't really my money to begin with.

"I'm sorry I missed it." She sniffs again. "I'm sorry about a lot of things."

I wonder if meeting me is one of those things. "I should have told you who I was."

Her face softens. "I didn't mean to react the way I did. It was just the suddenness of it all. I couldn't believe it was you, that boy . . ."

My jaw tightens. "You mean that freak?"

"The truth?"

"Yeah."

"I had a crush on you in kindergarten. But I remember that I was shy and you were the only one who was nice to me back then. Even if you were sort of different."

"Of course."

"I was five years old, Baxter. I can't control what I remember."

"You're not five years old now."

"And did you really think I was your soul mate? Wasn't I just an idea you romanticized?"

I stare at her. "You're not an idea. You're a person."

She sighs. "So you remembered me?"

"I remember that you had three freckles around your nose, that you hated the black tights your mom made you wear, that when you said the word 'spaghetti' it sounded like 'bas-ghetti,' that you wanted the condor I bought at the zoo that day." I stop and sigh. "I remember everything."

"Everything? As in *everything*?"

"Yes. Even stuff I want to forget."

"You must be the smartest guy in the world."

"Not really. There are a lot of things I don't know."

"Like what?"

"Like how to speak Portuguese or be a cork stripper."

Her mouth tilts in a half smile.

"Why didn't you tell me?" she asks.

I turn the book over in my hands. "Because you didn't remember me. I figured you'd like me better if I was someone else instead of the Memory Boy."

I want to cry, to beg her to feel the same way about me now that she felt before. I want to tell her it wasn't an accident that we moved here, that I've loved her since the first day I met her. But I know deep down that it's useless, and besides, I can't be that other person anymore.

"So you didn't give me a chance to know the real you." Her voice is harsh and I look up at her.

"Well, now you know the truth about Baxter Green," I say sarcastically.

She looks back at me, her brown eyes curious. "And what's that?"

"He's a pathetic loser."

Halle lets out a short breath. "Anyone who can memorize eighteen names and dates in a matter of seconds isn't a loser."

"Just a social outcast."

"Oh, no, nothing like that. Mysterious, maybe, like Gatsby. There are rumors about you. Some say you're an alien from outer space here to study life on earth. Others say you killed a man."

Is she teasing me or flirting? It's hard to tell with Halle. But for the first time in days I feel hopeful. It's time for some truth.

"Actually, I recited a thousand digits of pi in math class today. Eddie says I'm a superhero. Either that or a mutant."

Her eyes hold a spark of playfulness. "I vote for superhero. And we all know how difficult it is to have superpowers. Just look at Superman and Spider-Man. And by the way, Spider-Man was always forgetting his suit."

There's a breeze floating in from that small window of opportunity that Brad talked about. Halle is giving me another chance. But I have to be myself this time. Warts and all.

I clear my throat. "Akira Haraguchi said that memorization of pi was an expression of his lifelong quest for eternal truth."

"So his truth is in memorizing pi? Interesting."

"Of course, he took five-minute breaks every two hours to eat *onigiri* rice balls to keep up his energy levels."

"Well, of course. That always helps me."

"Do you remember the horse with two heads that you drew in kindergarten?"

"Are you kidding? I still have that drawing. It's framed on my wall."

"Um, you're joking, right?"

She nods. "I have absolutely no idea what you're talking about."

"Well, you did draw one. It was pretty amazing, really, considering that it was also biologically impossible, something I pointed out at the time." I stop. "By the way, feel free to tell me to shut up when I get too obnoxious."

Halle leans over and kisses me. "Oh, don't worry. You'll be the first to know," and the daffodils in her voice, lush and full, do a sexy little dance.

Memories

"Mom, we need to talk."

It's 6:21. She's just finished watching the weather segment of the news. There's a forecast for snow tonight and Mom is anxious. She's never driven in snow.

Dan Peterson helped her pick out special tires for the car and every day she watches the weather reports, ready to tackle her first Minnesota winter.

"I've been talking with Dr. Anderson," I say. "He'd like to do some more tests."

"You're not a guinea pig, Baxter. You don't have to do anything you don't want to do."

"I know. But maybe I want to do this."

"Oh. Really?" She sounds disappointed. "I thought you liked it here."

"I do. He's asked me to spend next summer at his research

facility in California. I could stay with Aunt Val. And Dr. Anderson even offered to let me stay at his house if I want. He's got a pool and a tennis court. He said he'd teach me how to play tennis."

"Tennis? What happened to the dragonflies?"

"I'm not really into . . ." Oh. She's teasing me. "Good one, Mom."

Mom ruffles my hair. "A whole summer without you?"

"You could come visit. Aunt Val would love to see you."

I'm hoping to talk Halle into coming, too. I don't think I could spend three months away from her, not after finding her again. But Mom doesn't even know that I'm dating Halle yet. That conversation is for another time.

Mom twirls a pencil in her fingers. I haven't caught her smoking in a week, but the pencil looks like it has teeth marks on it. "If that's what you really want to do."

Mom shivers and pulls on a sweater over her turtleneck shirt. She's learning how to dress in layers. Mom's also more fidgety since she's given up smoking. "You know, my memories aren't as good as yours. They're broken fragments, and pieces are missing. But they're good memories, at least most of them."

"I think that's the way memory is supposed to work."

"Sometimes, well, a lot of the time, I wish I had a better one."

"I used to hate remembering everything. But it would be weird to forget, too."

Mom looks thoughtful. "Well, I remember something you can't remember because you were too little. You were only two years old and Aunt Val and I took you to the zoo. You saw the giraffe and you wanted to know what kind of noise he made. I said he didn't make a noise. He just stuck out his long tongue to eat. So for the next two weeks you stuck out your tongue when you ate. Then you said you knew what sound the giraffe made."

"What sound was that?"

"You made this weird slurping sound. You said that all tongues made that noise, so that must be the sound the giraffe made. You spent the next week slurping your food every time you ate. I didn't take you to the zoo for a long time after that. See?" She smiles. "You don't remember everything."

"You're right. I don't remember that." I love it when I gain a new memory of my early years. It's like filling in pieces of a puzzle or adding one more stamp to a collection. I do remember that when I was older I found out that giraffes really do make noises.

So I search for a happy memory to give her in return. "Do you remember when you and dad took me trick-or-treating when I was three? It was two months after my fall on the playground."

She squints, as if the memory is out of reach, too far away.

"I wore a pirate costume with a patch over my eye and a bandanna on my head. I carried a cardboard sword that Dad had spray painted silver. Dad dressed up as Indiana Jones. He wore a leather jacket and a brown fedora pulled down over his eyes, and he carried a fake whip over his shoulder." I smile as the memory takes shape, and I remember how fearless I felt with my dad beside me.

"After Dad took me around the neighborhood, we came

back home and I rang our doorbell, thinking you wouldn't know it was me because I was wearing a costume. You pretended you didn't know who I was and gave me a Baby Ruth bar. You also said that Dad looked like Harrison Ford and you swooned and pretended to faint in the middle of the yard. Then Dad picked you up and carried you into the house." This is one of my favorite memories of them together.

One eyebrow goes up and Mom has a half smile on her lips. "I'd forgotten all about that." I can see her reconnecting the memory, maybe getting rid of an unpleasant Dink memory to make room for this happy one. Someday soon I'll tell her about Halle, and how sometimes people *can* get their happy endings. Mom is blushing, and in that instant, I feel as though the green light, the one that Gatsby watched from across a darkened sound, turns back on in Mom's heart.

I believe in the promise of that light.

Acknowledgments

Many thanks to the following people who were all involved in the making of my book: Stacy Cantor Abrams; Monica and Dave Barnes; Lisa Bullard; Mary Cummings; Emily Easton; Andrew, Brea, Brian, Chris, Erin, Jim, and Kasia Ellsworth; Steve and Vicki Palmquist; Luann Phillipich; Jane Resh Thomas; Robin Toboz; the Pheasant Writing Group; my Hamline University workshop group; Marsha Qualey; and the crew at Walker/Bloomsbury. If I've forgotten anyone, it's due to my poor memory.